CW01627255

Copyright © 2024 by Sara Amanda

All rights reserved

No part of this publication may be reproduced, distributed, or transmitted in any form or by any means, including photocopying, recording, or other electronic or mechanical methods, without the prior written permission of the publisher, except as permitted by EU copyright law. For permission requests, please contact the author.

The story, names, characters, and incidents portrayed in this production are fictitious, other than the ones clearly in the public domain. The companies and entities mentioned in this book have no affiliation with the author whatsoever.

Book Cover by Wonky Lines Book Cover Design

Line/ Copy Editing by Hannah G. Scheffer-Wentz, English Proper Editing Services

Proofreading by Katie Ducharme, Between The Covers Editorial LLC.

Created with Vellum

Dedication

To those of you who have lost a loved one without being lucky enough to say goodbye, to the ones who lost themselves in grief and anger, don't let it eat you alive.

Author's Note

The Wrong Palmer Boy is the first book in a duet. The story ends with a cliffhanger.

This book is intended for mature readers. The story contains the following topics that might be bothersome for some people:

- Bullying
- Su!cide (Not the MCs)
- Forbidden romance
- Death of a family member
- Dealing with grief
- Infidelity (Not the MCs. Their story does not contain cheating.)

Readers, if any of the above-mentioned topics trigger you, this book might not be for you.

Before you dive into Gigi and Luke's world, I want you to know that the characters are eighteen and twenty. Both of them will go through something terrible, but they are still young and some of their decisions will be immature.

Luke and Gigi's Playlist

Zach Bryan - Pink Skies
The Fray - How to Save a Life
Taylor Swift - This Love
Coldplay - The Scientist
Hozier - Like Real People Do
AJR - Weak
Taylor Swift - Guilty as Sin
Good Neighbours - Home
Benson Boone - Beautiful Things

Prologue

LUKE

EIGHTEEN YEARS OLD

CALL ME A SELF-CENTERED TEENAGER, CALL ME conceited, but when I packed up most of my belongings in the summer a few months ago, I thought I was responsible for the biggest shock that has ever happened to this family since the last one six years ago. I was sure, years from now, when people would talk about this year, they would talk about me and what I've done. How I broke the curse.

I mean, how could they not, right? The Palmers aren't known as a family who makes the good kind of waves, not the Palmers from Kinsdale Springs, anyway, but Lucas Palmer going to college? The son of Vincent Palmer, the tourist bus driver, being offered a full-ride scholarship to the University of Ravensfield? Please excuse my inflated ego, but after being told by one of my high school teachers that I should look into being a professional babysitter since I missed a lot of school during freshman year because Becca got sick a lot, an accomplishment like this is not something that I'm going to be humble about.

Well, I was wrong, because the biggest shock to the Palmer family this year is in the form of a female. Two of them, in fact. What's more unbelievable than the son from the wrong line of Palmers getting a scholarship? My dad getting remarried.

"Have you met them yet?" my second cousin and best friend, Andrew, asks me.

Sitting on the front porch steps, I nod. "Bianca has been here a few times." I honestly thought they would fizzle out at some point. That's usually what happens with most online relationships. *She's from New York, for fuck's sake.* The woman is, in all honesty, pretty nice. But why in the world would she move to a town in the middle of nowhere with a population of ten thousand?

"What about her daughter?"

"She brought her daughter along for the last two." I sigh, remembering how ridiculously upbeat Bianca's kid is. Honestly, she might be on drugs or something. Nobody is that happy in life.

"What's her name again? I forgot."

"Giuliana." With a mocking tone, I do my best to imitate her voice, and I say, "*But you can call her Gigi.*"

Andrew chuckles as he shakes his head. "Don't be an asshole, dude. You call yourself Luke and our brat doesn't go by Rebecca." *I hate it when he's right.* "I'm the only one that doesn't have a nickname. I kind of feel left out."

"Whatever. A little shit is what you are." He might not be little anymore, but he sure is a piece of shit for being the voice of reason. He's supposed to be on my side, not play Switzerland. But that's Andrew for you—always seeing the good in everything. Kind of like Gigi but less annoying.

"Here they come," he mumbles. His hand slaps my chest as he stands up. "Play nice."

I follow his gaze, and sure enough, I see my dad's truck

coming toward us. My sister sprints toward the car, almost knocking the breath out of me. The moment the back door opens and a leg slides down, Becca is already jumping up and down.

"Gigi! Gigi!" my seven-year-old sister squeals. "I'm so happy that you're here!"

It seems like I'm the only one immune to this girl's charms, because next to me, Andrew is clearing his throat. I groan when I see him adjust the bulge in his pants. *Sixteen-year-olds are idiots.* Pushing his chest forward, he saunters over to join the crowd. "Here, let me get this for you," he says to Giuliana. As he slings her backpack over one shoulder, his other hand reaches out for hers. "I'm Andrew Palmer. Lucas and Rebecca's second cousin."

I roll my eyes when I hear her answer. "Oh, hi! Thank you. I'm Giuliana, but you can call me Gigi." She flashes him a smile, and I've spent enough time with my cousin to know this much—that dude is a goner.

"Gigi, huh? I like it. We don't have many Gigis around here." Another eye roll.

"Are you also from here?" she asks Andrew. They're coming closer in my direction now, and I know that I have to mingle at some point. Might as well get it over with.

"He lives three towns over," I answer for him, standing up from my spot. "About one hour by car. Marble Crest." Since I don't have a legitimate reason to not like her, aside from the fact that she's prissy, I give her a curt smile before pulling her into a short hug. "Nice to see you again, Gigi. I hope the flight wasn't too rough."

Her gray eyes beam at my words. "Hi, Luke! Thanks for coming back home early. I thought we were only going to meet on Sunday. I'm so glad the three of us can bond before we officially become siblings." *It's not like I had a choice.*

"And me," Andrew decides to chime in. "I hang out here

all the time. I'm practically a bonus kid. Ask Luke." He looks at me, pleading with his eyes to vouch for him.

"He does," I confirm, but what I really want to do is smack his head so that the hearts in his eyes go away.

"Good to know, Andrew. We'll be seeing a lot more of each other, then," she says, batting her eyelashes. *Of course, she's flirting.*

"Here," he says, giving her his phone. The smile he's flashing her is making me cringe. "Give me your number. You could probably use a friend. Moving when the school year already started will probably suck. I might not live here, but I can show you around. A couple guys I know live here."

I'm getting second-hand embarrassment at how fast his crush on my soon-to-be stepsister is developing. The feeling turns into something I can't make out when I realize that they're the same age. She's going to move into my house. I know she doesn't know it yet, but the reason my dad told me to come back home a day earlier than the wedding is to move my shit out of my room and make space for hers. It's either that or she'd need to bunk with Becca and her dolls.

Will she take my spot as Andrew's best friend too? Will they date? He's certainly gunning for it. And fuck me, but they would actually make sense. The shiny new girl from New York and the golden Palmer boy from the respectable side of the family. I feel it in my bones. I was wrong. Me leaving this dump to better myself is not the catalyst to the Palmers changing. It's them.

CHAPTER 1
Gigi

ALMOST TWO YEARS LATER

Think of happy thoughts, Gigi. Picture the ocean. Picture the park. Picture Andrew kissing you in the dark.

I stand up. Hearing the echoes of my own heels click on the church floor, I make my way to the podium.

Think of happy thoughts, Gigi. Picture the ocean. Picture the park. Picture Andrew kissing you in the dark.

"Most of you have known Andrew longer than me," I read what I've written down on the index cards aloud. *The ones he got me when we were preparing for exams.* "Some of you have known Andrew his entire life. I wish I did." My voice breaks, and I feel a tear fall down on my left cheek. *The cheek he used to caress with his thumb.* "I wish I did, because two years were not enough to be able to say that I have spent enough time with Andrew Ethan Palmer. How do you say goodbye to the kindest blue eyes? To his warm laughter?"

Swallowing down the mental breakdown that's simmering, I finish my eulogy on autopilot. I think I hear some people clap. I think I see his parents smile. I think I feel Andrew here next to me when the wind breezes through the open side door.

Andrew would hate this—being the center of attention. If he could plan his own funeral, I bet he would do it differently. Maybe a small get-together instead of cramming everyone his family knows into a church, after this at the cemetery, and later at his house. By the end, he didn't even like half of the people who are here. He told me as much. Funny, how they all now claim to know him so well as they shake my hands and pull me into tight hugs.

Autopilot stops working the moment his old high school basketball coach decides to play a PowerPoint presentation in his living room. It's a slideshow of picture after picture of my boyfriend in his glory days—Andrew holding a trophy, Andrew having fun with his friends, Andrew focused, trying to make his shot. At the end of it, his former teammates who couldn't make it to today's funeral because they all just moved out of state for college a few weeks ago, appear one by one in separate videos. *We love you, Andrew. Let the eagles take you up high in the sky* is written on the last slide.

He looked so happy in all of the photos. I remember him being happy, too. I might have only had the luxury of knowing him for a blip in comparison to the others here, but I know one thing for sure—deep inside, Andrew Palmer was the human embodiment of a golden retriever. *What happened? How did we get here, Andrew?*

Think of happy thoughts, Gigi. Picture the ocean. Picture the park. Picture Andrew kissing you in the dark.

His friends all flock to me after that, gifting me with their condolences, as if their words mean anything. As if it would bring me comfort. As if it could resurrect him from the dead. I smile and nod. That's what you do, right? It's the polite thing. I can't exactly yell at them to shut up.

"I'm so sorry for your loss, Gigi," a familiar guy I've seen during orientation week on campus says, pulling me into yet another hug I didn't ask for. "I'm Zach. I used to go to school with Andrew. Saw you cheer when we played against Kinsdale Springs High once. I was on the football team."

"Thanks for coming," I mumble.

Think of happy thoughts, Gigi. Picture the ocean. Picture the park. Picture Andrew kissing you in the dark.

Seeing Zach is my cue to find some air. He's the living proof that this is not just some fucked up joke. By the time I'm back in Ravensfield, the nightmare will continue. Andrew and I might have not been freshmen long enough to make friends yet, but I'm not kidding myself—people will start to approach me after this, their wandering minds getting the best of them. Everyone will gossip about us.

They won't talk about how he was so excited to go to college, how he made a geeky bucket list for things to do in Ravensfield. They won't ask me questions about how cheesy his prom-posal was. They won't care about how we overcame our rough patch together as a couple. No. They will come to me to pump me for information and run their mouths about one thing, and one thing only. They don't want to know us, not really. They're just curious about the guy who was found in his dorm room. *And the girlfriend that he left behind.*

Think of happy thoughts, Gigi. Picture the ocean. Picture the park. Picture Andrew kissing you in the dark.

"Let me have a sip," I say when I spot Luke all alone on the dimly lit back porch, holding a tumbler of amber liquid. My stepbrother despises big gatherings, and for the first time in my life, I understand the appeal.

Luke cocks an eyebrow. "No," he says as he brings his drink closer to him, taking another sip.

"I'm not here to fight, Luke."

"And I'm not Andrew. I don't bend to your every will." He turns on his heel and walks away.

I could have said something—a nasty comeback, a snide comment—but I don't. I let him go. Most people wouldn't let it slide, mourning girlfriends probably shouldn't. I normally don't. It's because I get him.

By the way he's already drunk at 7:00 p.m., noticing his rumpled, button-down shirt, seeing how disheveled he looks... Luke is suffering. The heart-cracked-in-two type.

If there is one person that I pity more than Andrew's parents and myself, it's him. Once upon a time, two boys spent all their free time and summers together, despite the fact that the only similarities they shared were their last name and the same dirty blond hair color. It all changed when Luke left for Ravensfield. Andrew going to the same college was supposed to be a new start for the both of them. I might have lost my boyfriend, but Luke lost the person who he probably loved the most.

CHAPTER 2

Luke

EIGHTEEN YEARS. EIGHTEEN AND A HALF YEARS, TO be exact. That's how long I have spent walking on this Earth knowing Andrew. The only time I've lived on this Earth without him existing is when I was wearing diapers. How do I spend my life knowing that I can never fucking call him again? How do I walk around campus knowing that he should be there with me? How do I go back home every summer knowing I can't just drive up and find him shooting hoops in the driveway of his house?

They say the first stage of grief is denial. I think I might have skipped that one, because all I feel is anger. When I found him the way I did, I knew for certain what he had done. I wasn't delusional about it. Gigi was the one who was deluding herself into thinking there had been a mistake.

"Shit," I groan when I realize that I have to apologize to her now.

What I said to her at his house? Even I know that was uncalled for. Gigi doesn't deserve that. For all her flaws and my reservations about her, I think she really did love him. He loved her, too, which makes everything even more fucked up.

Andrew had everything any eighteen-year-old could have possibly wanted—the jock life, a pretty girlfriend, loving parents, zero money problems, and a chance to study what he wanted. He also had me. Things weren't the same after he started dating Gigi and I was in college, but I was always only a phone call away.

What the fuck, Andrew?

Knowing I will probably punch a wall if I don't stop overusing my brain thinking about *what-ifs,* I yank open the door of my old bedroom and take ten steps until I reach Becca's. My stepsister comes out after a few knocks.

"She's already asleep," Gigi whispers, gripping the door with her hand. "What's up?"

"Did I wake you?"

"I was on my phone." With her eyes so red and her nose puffy, any idiot can tell that she was probably crying just five seconds ago. "What do you need, Luke?"

"You can have your room," I tell her. "I'll take the air mattress." I would've done it, anyway, but she got home a day before me when her mom picked her up from campus. When I arrived, Gigi had already set up camp in my sister's room.

"It's yours. Besides, I miss Becca."

"I'm sorry," I blurt out.

"I know," she answers with her eyes facing the floor.

"I didn't mean it. I'm just...I don't know."

She smiles. I haven't seen the sight in a while. "I know how you feel. I'm just I don't know, too."

A silent moment passes. Unspoken words drifting through the air.

I miss him. I miss him, too.

How could he do this? I don't know.

Why didn't we realize anything? He wasn't showing any signs.

"Alright, you really don't want the room?" I ask, just to be sure.

"Have a good night, Luke."

"You, too." The sound of her voice...It's always chirpy and light. This time, though, she doesn't have the expression that usually goes along with it.

Five minutes later, I'm back in my room. Her room now, I suppose. The band posters are now replaced with her framed pictures from high school. The biggest one, a picture of her and her squad in green and white cheerleading outfits with matching colored pom poms, stares back at me from above her bed. I don't even try to redirect my train of thoughts when it goes straight to Andrew. The cheerleader and the athlete. A teenager's dream come true. Did they go to each other's games? Alternating between football and basketball? Was that how my cousin lived the last year of his life?

Walking around, my urge to snoop gets stronger. It's interesting what she has done with the place. *And of course, Gigi would have a live, laugh, love poster above her desk.*

When my eyes trail down, I spot a red, rectangular tin. I almost stop with the creeping. Almost. But then I open the lid, and I see him. It must be their memento box or some shit. Autumn, my ex from sophomore year of college, used to keep something like this. The contents are also similar. I shuffle through the tens of pictures of them inside. Gigi also keeps countless ticket stubs from the only movie theater in the area. I feel the darkness leaving my body for a little bit once I hold a Polaroid photo of the two of them in a bowling alley. *He looked happy.*

I'm about to close the box and leave the memories of them alone when I see something taped to the lid. An envelope. *I'm already going through everything, anyway, so I might as well.* Since this is the only way I can get close to my cousin now, I disrespect her privacy once again. What I find written down doesn't only bring back the darkness, but morphs whatever I was feeling into full-blown rage.

Dear Gigi,

I hate that we're fighting, and I hate that you're ignoring my calls and texts. They created phones for a reason, you know? I tried looking for a carrier pigeon, but apparently, we don't have those anymore. So flowers and a good old fashioned letter, it is.

I know we're not great right now, but it's going to be better, I promise. I'm going to be better. I'm miserable and I need you, Gigi. The past two weeks have been hell.

I'm so, so, so sorry.

Please don't break up with me. I don't know what I'd do without you. I'd probably have to jump off a bridge or something.

Your very hot, very sorry boyfriend,

Andrew

To a lot of people, *jumping of a bridge* is a fucking figure of speech. No one ever means it. Until they do, that is. My fists curl into balls as my mind goes over a hundred miles an hour. What happened to these two? Is she the reason why? I might have a lot of questions, but I know one thing is for sure. I will get to the bottom of it.

I thought Giuliana Bankowski would make *my life* a living hell the moment she waltzed into our lives. Maybe I was wrong. Maybe it was Andrew's.

CHAPTER 3

Gigi

THIS YEAR'S CHRISTMAS DIDN'T GO AS PLANNED. Well, that's an understatement. Nothing this year has gone as planned. *And nothing will.*

Andrew and I wanted to spend it with his parents. They have been hounding him ever since we drove to Ravensfield that we should stay at their place instead of with my mom and Luke's dad. It made perfect sense—Luke would get his own room to crash in and we would drive back and forth. Funny, isn't it? Giuliana, Miss Planning-everything-down-to-a-T as my mom likes to call me, is slowly figuring out that life doesn't always go how you want it. No matter how much you prepare everything with Excel spreadsheets.

I feel pricking in the back of my eyes thinking about him. Something that has been happening way too often lately. *Why did you even make plans if you knew that you weren't going to do it, Andrew? Why did you even go to college if you were planning on not being there anymore the next month?*

I decided to take my dad up on his offer and spend my winter break with him in New York. As a matter of fact, I also spent Thanksgiving break with him. It felt good to be back.

My mother used to hate living in Greenpoint. It bothered her that we were living next door to my paternal grandparents. Although I'd be the first one to admit that they sometimes can be overwhelming, I don't mind it as much, especially this time. They knew not to speak of what happened, choosing to stuff my mouth with homemade perogies, instead.

I doubt Andrew's parents would still have wanted me there, anyway. My mom likes to update me during our calls. With the way the both of them have completely shut down, I don't think they'd want an audience to the downfall of their lives. The most perfect Palmer family, cracking.

The other Palmer family, the one who people rarely talk about nowadays—*my Palmers*—wasn't too happy about my decision to go to Dad's. Everyone except Luke, I bet. He's also not talking to me anymore. We were never close, but he downright only speaks in grunts and nods whenever he sees me on campus now. I can't help but think that he feels a little guilty for abandoning Andrew after he moved to Ravensfield, and maybe I'm a reminder of that. One day they were attached at the hip, and the next Luke barely drives home anymore. A two-hour drive is not too long if you really want to see your best friend.

Think of happy thoughts, Gigi. Picture the ocean. Picture the park. Picture Andrew kissing you in the dark.

Slinging my backpack over my shoulder, I make my way to the front entrance of my dorm. Polite *hellos* and *how are yous* greet me. I give them my smile, but it's getting faker by the day. By the time I reach my room, I breathe out a sigh of relief, happy to finally be confined within four white walls. Away from these strangers who I never got a chance to befriend. Meeting new people used to exhilarate me. Now I just want to be left alone.

"Hi, Gigi," my roommate Zoey says. "How was winter break?"

"It was alright." I drop all my luggage and give her a hug. A genuine one for my only friend here. "I missed you, though."

"Girl, you see me every day."

"And I love every second of it." I give her a wink.

Besides Andrew, I have only ever spent time with Zoey here ever since the start of freshman year. How I got so lucky to have her as a roommate, I have no fucking clue. But Zoey has been amazing with her support, despite not knowing me for that long. From fending off vultures who just want to get the gossip straight from the source, to thinking about me when she gets takeout, she has more than earned the best friend title. Come to think of it, none of the girls from my high school cheer squad are as nice as her.

"Soooo," Zoey hums, her eyes pleading and hopeful for something. I don't know what yet, but I can guess.

"What do you need, Zoey?"

"Zach invited us to a party." *There it is*. When I give her a sigh as a response, her brown orbs beg some more. Like a puppy wanting a new chew toy. "Please? I really like his roommate."

"For the record, I'm only going because I love the two of you." It feels wrong to have fun. To go to a party and sip from a red solo cup like I'm a normal eighteen-year-old without a care in the world. But Zach and Zoey, the two Zs, as I like to call them in my head, have been supporting me ever since they showed up to Andrew's funeral.

"Good girl," she squeals. With a softened expression on her face, Zoey continues, "You deserve this, Gigi."

It has been three and a half months now. *Maybe I do. Maybe I'll try.*

I'm putting on my lipstick when my phone buzzes in my pocket. Smiling, I already know who it's from.

ZACH

Heard from Zoey you're coming out tonight. Did all the ice in Antarctica melt? Did the sun set in the west?

The sun does set in the west, you idiot.

I shake my head, laughing, continuing with my makeup. I didn't know Zach before college. Not personally, at least. Andrew played basketball and Zach was a football player. The two teams in their school, like in your stereotypical, stupid teen drama, have some long-standing beef. Not bad enough to cause fistfights, but serious enough that the moment you make it past the tryouts, you stop running in the same circles and going to the same parties with the people from the other one. If Andrew could see this, he would laugh that I'm now friends with Zach. He always thought the rivalry was stupid.

Another message comes through as I'm calling my mother, giving her my weekly updates and trying to convince her that I'm not depressed.

ZACH

Okay, smartass. We'll pick you girls up in five. You ready for your first frat party?

Think of happy thoughts, Gigi. Picture the ocean. Picture the park. Picture Andrew kissing you in the dark.

I can do this.

CHAPTER 4
Luke

"BRO, CAN YOU BE THE DESIGNATED DRIVER?" MY friend Kai yells from the kitchen.

"Yeah, no problem."

Although I would love nothing more than to drink my weight in booze tonight to forget about the winter break from hell, I kind of owe Kai this one. Ever since Andrew died, he has been through it. And by *it*, I mean me. I was a horrible fucking roommate to have. The both of us had to patch up the holes I punched in the wall at some point. Good thing I'm already over the anger stage of my grief. Now...now I just feel numb. And I wonder if it will always be like this. *Will I not care about anything anymore? Forever?* It's better than caring too much, I guess.

Autumn curls up next to me on the couch, already pregaming with a beer in hand. From this angle, I can see the way her breasts move with each breath she takes. I remember when I used to get so turned on by a sneak peek of her tits. Everything, including my dating life, just feels so insignificant. How could they not? In the grand scheme of things, who I fuck in college doesn't matter. What I study doesn't really matter. People are born, they live, and they die. All the time. I'm just one out of many. I could be out like a light tomorrow, and what happens tonight won't be remembered by anybody.

"You sure you don't want to drink?" Autumn asks me.

"Yeah, It's fine. I haven't been the designated driver in a while. Kai has been cutting me some slack." A lot of slack. *Shit ton.*

"You want to do something else later to relax?" Autumn is observing me, trying to gauge my reaction. I already know where this is going, and I don't like it one bit.

"Look," I say, closing my eyes. "What happened was a one-time thing, okay?" And I'll be damned if it were to happen again. There was a reason why we broke up in the first place. Me reaching out to her last week? That was a moment of weakness.

"Alright, you two ready?" Malakai shows up in the living room, a big smile plastered on his face, completely oblivious to the disappointment of my ex-girlfriend.

❧

In forty years' time, all of the people in this frat house, me included, will be deaf. Mark my words. I would bet my nonexistent trust fund on it. Either deaf or dying of liver disease.

"What?" I scream to Kai. With how loud the bass is thumping, I'm not even sure he hears me.

"I said, do you want to get wasted? Toby is not drinking tonight. Got a quiz or some shit tomorrow," he replies in a volume matching mine.

When you're in college and constantly hanging around a bunch of other guys, the probability of them knowing how to help you navigate through loss is pretty low. I'm pretty sure my friends' love language is binge drinking. Either that or video games. Fortunately for them, I'm happy to go along with that.

"Kitchen, then, yeah?" Kai grins at the mention of the kitchen, then makes his way to the place where an ample supply of alcohol is being served with me in tow.

Four tequila shots later, I finally spot the empty Amarula bottle on the counter hidden between the dirty dishes. For the first time in a long while, I smile. Andrew and his parents went to South Africa when he was fourteen. They brought back two bottles of the cream liqueur they got as gifts. Other kids had beer as their first taste of alcohol, but not him. Not Andrew. He was adamant about trying this horrible-tasting shit. He made me the lookout as he poured some into two coffee mugs.

I hate the fact that the only thing that seems to be able to make me feel an inkling of happiness is also the thing that makes me want to turn off all the lights in my room and curl into a fetal position, drowning out the outside noise. *Memories of my dead cousin.*

"So, are you and Autumn back together, or what?" Kai asks before drinking the contents of his red cup dry.

"Nope." Even if I was in the right headspace for a relationship right now, I will not go down the Autumn road again. Autumn might have some people fooled with the small tattoos scattered all over her body and her penchant for being one of the guys, but one weekend in her hometown to meet her folks was enough to figure out who she was.

"Whatever you say, man." Kai chuckles as he gives me a tap on the shoulder. He pauses before he speaks again, in between sips of the beer he just cracked open. "That girl looks hot."

"You can't even see her face, you pig," I sneer. "Dude, the only thing you can see is her ass. I see what you mean, though. I bet she's pretty, too." I can't blame Kai for checking her out. The way the girl's jeans hug her curves, no wonder the group of guys standing next to her is dying to insert themselves in whatever conversation she's got going on.

"No, not her." With the hand that's holding the beer bottle, Kai uses his index finger to point at a girl standing next to the person I thought was the one. Before I can get a look at her, Kai nods his head and strides over to them. "Come on, let's say hi," he says with a shit-eating grin on his face.

"Hello, ladies," Kai announces from the back. "My name is Malakai and this is my friend—"

"Hi, Luke," Kai's prey for the night greets me. Zelda, maybe? I met her at the funeral. I think she's Andrew's friend. She wasn't sporting a pixie cut back then.

I feel like I'm about to pass out when the other girl turns her head around to face me. "Oh! Hi," she says with a smile on her face. "Fancy seeing you here."

Gigi.

Giuliana Bankowski.

My stepsister.

I can't believe I was just checking out my stepsister's ass.

I can't believe I was just checking out Andrew's girlfriend's ass.

I feel disgusted that I was watching the way Gigi's hips swayed in those jeans, following the rhythm coming out of the speakers. *Fuck me, I'm drunk.*

"You both cut your hair," is all I can get out.

Gigi and her friend, who I now remember is called Zoey, both look at each other, staring at the pixie cut and the bob that replace the long locks that used to frame their faces.

"Yeah, we did," one of them says, but I'm too busy trying to mentally bleach my brain to focus on who's speaking. "New year, new us!"

"How do you guys know Luke?" Kai eyes the three of us curiously. *Seems like he doesn't recognize them, either.*

"Oh, he's my stepbrother," Gigi answers.

Kai nods slowly, and suddenly he has a look on his face like he's holding in a laugh. He's wise not to react to the comment. He might not have known Andrew personally, but he has heard enough of my drunken rants to know who he was, who he dated, and what happened. Plus, he was there that night. Shooing people the fuck away.

Before any of us can say anything else, four frat guys come out of the kitchen holding small, clear, plastic cups with yellow blobs inside. "Jell-O shots!"

And I take two immediately. All for me. Tonight is about to get fucking weird, and I don't want to deal with whatever's going to happen sober. Not if I can help it.

CHAPTER 5
Gigi

THANK THE LORD THAT WE BUMPED INTO LUKE AND his friend, Malakai. Zach and Zoey have been pushing me to go out there and start dating again, with Zach basically serving me on a silver platter to any of his football friends who spare me a second glance.

With Zoey and Malakai flirting with each other as if no one is looking, basically undressing the other person with their eyes, I'm pretty sure I'm going to be stuck with Luke until these two get a room. At least this way, I know nothing is going to happen. No small talk with randos asking me what my favorite color is or where I come from, when they actually don't care and just want to get me out of my pants.

"You two want to head back to our place?" Kai asks, but his eyes only focus on one person, and it's not me. "The party is pretty much dead now, anyway." I do a quick sweep of my surroundings. Sure enough, people are starting to zip up their coats or throw up in potted plants.

"Absolutely. We would love to," Zoey answers for the both of us. She looks at me for reassurance, and I answer with my face that's trying to say, *go get it, girl.*

"Where do you guys live?" I ask the guys.

"Not far from here," Luke answers.

Kai, the sweet to his sour, gives me something more detailed. "We live off-campus on Covington Street. Just five blocks away." Kai looks around the house before turning to Luke and says, "I think Toby bailed on us, man. Looks like we're walking."

The moment we walk out, the cold breeze slaps my cheek. I haven't been to a party in such a long time, I forgot what it feels like to walk outside at two in the morning. The copious amount of alcohol I just consumed is not helping to warm me up.

Zoey is torn between continuing to walk beside me, with us linked together, or walking next to Kai. I decide to relieve them both of their misery and unhook my arms from her, letting her go to the guy with dreamy eyes. Just because I won't be getting any doesn't mean she has to suffer the same fate.

With the two of them hand in hand, I'm at the back of the group. My feet try to keep up with their pace, but the pavement is glazed with ice and my heeled boots are not helping. Just as I am about to hit my ass on the ground, Luke, by some miracle, turns his head around and approaches me in two big strides.

"Jesus," he mutters. "How much did you have to drink?"

Luke lets me hold his arm so that I can prop myself up, and I think this is the most contact we've had in a long time. Tonight has been the most interaction I've had with him since we met, actually. He rarely comes home from college, and when he does, I'm usually in New York, visiting my dad.

"It's not that. It's the shoes." I bend one of my legs and lift it up slightly to make a point, showing him the heel.

"You couldn't wear sneakers like a normal person?" His

tone is condescending, and usually, I let it slide. But tonight, liquid courage is fueling me.

"You couldn't just walk next to me like a normal person?" I scoff.

He stares at me, momentarily halting his steps like he can't believe that I just answered back. Once the shock wears off, he shoves both of his hands in his pockets. I don't miss the way he adjusts to my steps, though. "It's not my fault you have short legs, Gi."

"It's not my fault yours are freakishly long, Luke. What are you? Bigfoot? You sure are as fucking scary as him." I sound like I mean what I'm saying, but it couldn't be further from the truth. Luke doesn't look like a freakishly tall monster who lurks in the shadows. He looks exactly like what he is. With his hair now slightly longer than a buzz cut and his honey eyes, my stepbrother is your typical boy next door that girls, good or bad, crush hard for. According to Andrew, he has the personality to back it up, too. Personally, I have never seen him live up to that claim.

Luke bites his lips, trying to hide the smile that's forming. The Jell-O shots must be kicking in, because I decide to open my mouth again. "Oh, just laugh if you want to, Luke. God forbid, Gigi actually said something funny or cute."

He rolls his eyes, but at least he's letting his lips quirk naturally now. "You're annoying. Do you know that?"

"Right back at you."

After a few minutes of walking next to each other in silence, we stop in front of a five-story building. I see Luke's car in one of the parking spaces, covered in a coat of snow. Memories flash in my head of the day I moved to Ravensfield. Andrew and I couldn't fit all of our belongings in his hatchback, my mom's Smart car, and his dad's sedan. For some bizarre reason, Luke's father had to force him into bringing a few of my boxes here. Luke didn't say anything in particular, he never does, but he acted like helping me transport my things in the empty backseat of his car was doing a favor for the devil himself.

When Kai fumbles with his keys, clearly distracted by the full-blown make-out session he's having with Zoey, Luke grunts and shoves him out of the way. He reaches into the back pocket of his jeans and pulls out his own set, opening the door for us.

The two lovebirds don't waste any time after the awkward elevator ride up to the second floor. They spare us no second glances and immediately close the door to what must be Kai's room. I probably would do the same. *These two are practically family, right? They know how to spend time with each other,* is what they probably are thinking right now.

"Nice place," I mumble to Luke, not knowing what else to say. The empty cans of soda, beer, and energy drinks on the coffee table aside, their apartment looks pretty decent for a place inhabited by two twenty-year-olds. My dorm room is messier than this.

Luke takes off his baseball cap, giving me a glimpse of the same dirty blond shade that all the Palmers seem to inherit through the bloodline. He runs his hand through the back of his head before resting it on his neck, seemingly unsure of what to do with me invading his space.

"I'll, uh, I'll get you a pair of sweatpants," he finally says. "If you want."

"Why?" I ask with a cocked eyebrow.

"I don't think Zoey and Kai will be done anytime soon," he deadpans.

"I mean why are you being so nice to me? You offering me something so that I'm comfortable is out of character. You love to see me suffer, don't you dare deny it."

A smirk comes out of him as he crosses his hands over his

chest. "Well, well, well. It seems like Little Miss Sunshine has claws, after all."

And they come out when I'm drunk. I feel the temperature in me slowly rising, and I don't know if it's due to two years' worth of frustration or if my body is finally reacting to the heating in this apartment. "Whatever fucking problem you have with me, Luke. Just spit it out. I know you don't like me."

Luke's jaw ticks and his honey-colored eyes look at me with disdain. "Oh, I don't like you, alright." The second he opens his mouth again, I immediately regret poking the bear. "I know about the letter. I saw what Andrew wrote."

Suddenly, I'm hit with the emotions all at once. Grief, sadness, embarrassment, and a sobering dose of faltering self-confidence.

"Luke, let me explain."

Think of happy thoughts, Gigi. Picture the ocean. Picture the park. Picture Andrew kissing you in the dark.

The secret of a dead man.

CHAPTER 6
Luke

Gigi's eyes are giving me a glimpse into her mind. Stormy gray, troubled, and having a problem staying still. I bet her brain is churning, trying to figure out how to get herself out of this situation.

"*Please*," I say in a mocking tone as I open the door to my room, willing her to follow me so that Kai and Zoey don't hear us. "Explain how you sunk your claws into Andrew and ruined his life."

"I didn't." She closes her eyes, her lips in a tight line. Gigi takes three deep breaths before opening them again. "I didn't ruin his life, Luke."

My fist curls when I remember what was on that letter.

Please don't break up with me. I don't know what I would do without you. I'd probably have to jump off a bridge or something.

"But you knew he was having problems."

Again, Gigi takes deep breaths. "I didn't know. Luke, please, you have to believe me." Her voice is breaking.

Considering how drunk we both are right now, I'm pretty sure nothing good will come out of this fight, but grief is a funny thing. It has a mind of its own. "That's bullshit, Gi. He basically spelled it out for you. And you didn't do a goddamn thing!"

Opening my closet, I pull out a pair of sweatpants and a hoodie. They're for me. I gather both items in my hands, holding them in a rumpled ball. A giant stress ball so that I don't punch another hole in the wall. I'm halfway out the door, about to shower and leave her in her spot when Gigi says something that makes me freeze in position.

"The letter had nothing to do with that. He...he slept with somebody else." Her voice is croaked, and I bet if I look at her, I can see tears. "But we made up. We were fine."

"You're lying."

"I'm not."

"You are." He would never. We might not have been that close in blood, but I know him. He was my best friend. Andrew was the boyfriend equivalent of a soft baked, chocolate chip cookie. The kind your mother makes during the Christmas season. No hard edges, gooey, sweet. Makes everyone happy and your teeth ache. Goddamn perfect.

As a family, he was the same. I'm proof of that. When everyone kept on comparing us because we were of similar age, Andrew always changed the topic. When my dad shut down and the only job he could hold down was the one that would take him away from me and Becca for long periods of time, Andrew and his family rallied around and begged people who knew us to babysit Becca in rotation, knowing that we were too proud to ask for help.

As a friend, he never once listened to his athlete friends when they questioned his decision to hang out with me. Andrew always hung out at my house, even though his place was three times the size, knowing that it made me uncomfortable to be at his home. Knowing that it was too far of a bike ride to go there.

I turn on my heel, facing Gigi and fighting the urge to shake some sense into her. "Don't you dare lie about shit like that. Not about him!" I yell.

She takes a step back, the gray orbs turning scared. Yet undeterred, Gigi sticks with her story. "Defend him all you want, Luke. It's the truth. Stop acting like you've been around to know what he was like."

"Say I believe your delusion. Who was the girl, huh?"

"Rachel."

The laugh I bark out startles her. *God, she's so pathetic.* "This is how I know you're definitely lying. Rachel from church? You seriously want me to believe that my cousin cheated on you with Rachel from his church? Are you out of your fucking mind?"

"It's fucking true!" she screams through her cries, strands of her dark hair sticking to her wet face. Why she's continuing to stand on this faltering house of lies, I have no clue.

"I've known Rachel since I was a child, Gi. I've lived in that dumphole longer than you. There is no way that happened."

Andrew. The son of the pastor. Stepping out on his girlfriend with Rachel from church. Andrew's not squeaky clean, but he's not that bad, either. Gigi should be a screenwriter. A sitcom is what this is.

"Then what do you think happened?" She throws a question back. "If you're so sure Andrew didn't cheat on me, why did you think he wrote that letter?"

That's a good fucking point, but I'm far too angry to give her a pat on the back for pointing that out. "You probably got mad at him for something stupid and overreacted," I say after deliberating. "I expect no less from someone as high-maintenance as you. Or maybe *you* were the one who cheated and fucking gaslit him."

Gigi flashes me a smile that doesn't reach her eyes, turning her head to the side so she doesn't have to look at me. I don't need to see her full profile to know how she's feeling. The heartbreak can be seen from the moon. Suddenly, I get a sinking feeling in my stomach telling me that, possibly, I took it too far.

"You don't know me, asshole. You never even tried to get to know me, so don't make assumptions." She sprints out of my room and a few seconds later, I hear the slam of the front door.

Dead people can't talk, but if Andrew were still alive, what would he say to me? Guilty or not guilty, how would he feel if I told him that I just kicked her while she was down?

CHAPTER 7
Gigi

Think of happy thoughts, Gigi. Picture the ocean. Picture the park. Picture Andrew kissing you in the dark.

I shake my head, quickly erasing the thought in my head. I suppose the last chant in my mantra wouldn't be fitting for what I'm about to do.

Checking my phone one last time, I decide to send a message to the guy responsible for today.

Wish me luck. I'm here now waiting.

ZACH

It's going to be great. You have a lot in common.

I'm about to close the messaging app, but then I see Zoey's name underneath Zach's. Smiling, I type out another text.

I'm so fucking nervous right now. He's going to see armpit stains.

ZOEY

Do you have a cardigan with you?

Good thinking. I grab my black cardigan that's draped over the chair I'm sitting on. The one I bought on sale last Black Friday with the gift card Mom sent me. I've been spending all of my holidays with Dad in New York, so the gift exchange Mom and I have been doing is in the form of emails. As I'm putting my arm inside the hole, a finger taps on my shoulder.

"Are you Gigi?" the guy with the lazy smile asks. Wow, Zach wasn't kidding when he mentioned that his friend is easy on the eyes. Muscular build. Intense mocha eyes. A French accent. Not a bad way to kick off my return to the dating world. You can tell a lot about a person by the sound of their voice. Granted, he has only said three words to me, but I think he might have the personality to match his physical attractiveness. *Or maybe you've been alone for way too long and highly inexperienced, Gigi.*

"Pierre, right?" I ask, pushing myself to stand up so that I can shake his hand.

He doesn't take the palm I'm offering him, because at the same time, his arms form half a circle. We're stuck in this awkward should-we-shake-hands-or-should-we-hug standstill before laughter erupts out of us both.

Zach's friend pulls me into a light embrace, one appropriate for two people who just met three seconds ago, and claims the seat on the opposite side of the small round table.

"So Gigi...what is it short for?"

I grin. *I can do this. This one is easy.* "Giuliana Bankowski." When he doesn't raise an eyebrow in surprise like some people, I decide to elaborate anyway and give him the play-by-play. "My mom is Italian and my dad is Polish."

Another lazy smile slowly creases on his lips. When said lips start talking, I finally get his lack of reaction. "Pierre Adebayo," he says, holding his hand to his button-down clad chest while leaning closer to the table. "French mom and Nigerian dad."

It turns out, Zach is not that bad at matchmaking after all. Maybe he should put his business degree to good use.

"Well, hello there, fellow multicultural child." The flirtiness in my tone surprises me.

"Zach didn't tell me you were also mixed," he replies.

"I have two white parents, that's hardly a mixture." I laugh along with him, but inside, my heart is starting to hammer in my chest. "What else did, uh, Zach tell you about me?" I ask in the most relaxed way I can possibly try to fake.

"Nothing much." He shrugs. He pauses for a second when the waiter comes with our orders that we placed at the counter. Leaning back on his chair as he drapes an arm over the backrest, he continues, "Just that you study psychology and come from his hometown."

I make a mental note to thank Zach for keeping his lips shut tight. According to him, Pierre is a twenty-one-year-old exchange student who just arrived in Ravensfield. By the time the snow had set in, students had moved on to the next big scandal that graced this small college town—a drunk sorority sister who got so drunk she decided to bring a professor she was screwing to a party. I can't say I was sad when people started talking about her instead of me.

"Not the same town, actually," I clarify. "Three towns over, if we're being exact. Actually, scratch that. I'm originally from New York, but I moved to Kinsdale Springs when my mom remarried. Zach is from Marble Crest." *God, that's a lot of oversharing.* "What about you? I heard you just came here. How are you liking the States so far?"

"Ravensfield is different than Lyon, that's for sure," he says, his dark eyes looking up as he takes a bite from his muffin.

"Less fancy?"

He laughs. "Yes, less fancy. And very small. But everyone is very friendly here. I like it. So tell me a bit about yourself."

Our blabbering continues on and on. I tell him about my firefighter dad, and he tells me about his bio dad who's a teacher, as well as his stepfather who is currently here as a visiting professor at the University of Ravensfield. I tell him about my nurse mom and he volleys back with a story of how his mom is bored out of her mind, always using every opportunity to count down the days until the six-month period of their stay here is over. He tells me he came here when his stepdad offered because it would look good on his résumé, and I explain to him that I took out a student loan to be able to go here, supplementing my living costs with waitressing.

The conversation flows naturally—easy laughter, friendly banter. I make sure that I don't trauma dump and keep everything light. When he walks me back to my dorm, Pierre gives me another hug, less awkward this time. He doesn't ask for a second date or promise to call me once he gets home. I don't, either.

Some people would view the lack of chemistry between us and my failure to snag the hottie as an unsuccessful date, but they couldn't be more wrong.

Today proved something to me: one, today feels nice. Although Pierre probably isn't the one, getting back out there feels right. Two, I'm easygoing. *Fuck Luke and his comment about me being high-maintenance. You know what? Fuck Luke, period*

CHAPTER 8
Luke

IT'S BEEN THREE WEEKS SINCE I LAST SAW HER, BUT I can't get Gigi out of my head. Can't get what I said to her out of my head. My right knee bobs up and down thinking about the fucked up shit that came out of my mouth. *Was I out of line? I definitely was. I should probably apologize.*

"Dude, cool it," somebody hisses from the table next to me.

I turn my head and the semi-permanent scowl that's on my face forms itself. "What's your problem?"

"Your stupid fucking pen. Some of us are trying to study."

I follow his line of sight and, sure enough, find my hand clicking my pen repeatedly. I nod. "Sorry." The guy shakes his head, and I turn mine back, my focus now on the scattered blue dots on the corner of my textbook. *I'm not above apologizing. I can admit when I'm wrong.*

Not even ten minutes of diving back into the world of accounting, I hear the door to the library open. Autumn comes in holding an insulated travel mug in one hand and the same textbook I have open in front of me in the other. Walking like she owns the place, like she owns me, she puts the two items down on the table and my backpack on the floor, freeing the chair next to mine.

"The auditing module is messing with my head," she says casually as she grabs my water bottle and twists the cap open. *You're messing with my head.*

"That's mine, Autumn."

She looks at me wide-eyed, but drinks from it anyway to make a point. "What? You're too good to swap spit with me now?"

I vocalize the hundreds of groans I've been making in my head ever since she fucking waltzed in here, shaking my head as I do so. "Please, I'm trying to focus here, Autumn. I'm already on thin ice as it is with my scholarship."

"I miss you, babe."

My molars grit against each other hard. "Don't." Autumn grabs my forearm. The feel of her fingers causes bile to rise up to my throat.

Not going down without a fight, Autumn moves her hand to my thigh. "I want us to get back together, Luke."

There's nothing else to do but laugh at this point. "I'm done with this," I whisper since the guy behind me is looking angry all over again. I should have studied somewhere else today; the guy would have had a much more peaceful time, and I wouldn't have to deal with this crap.

"But...you were the one who started again, Luke." *She has a point.* "You sought me out." Autumn works her hand to my inner thigh, gripping the flesh lightly, knowing I like this.

"It was a one-time thing," I say through gritted teeth, prying her fingers off me. "Now leave me alone. Please."

"Is there someone else?" *Oh, come fucking on.*

"That's really rich coming from you." I close my textbook and pack up my shit. Not staying here for this bullshit.

"Luke, please," she begs with the blue doe eyes that once made me weak in the knees. The ones that made me dare to think I was worthy of someone like her. "I still want to be with you."

"Autumn." I close my eyes and count to five in my head. "Maybe you should have thought about that before going back to Asher."

I don't let her answer. Instead, I put on my coat and make my way back to my place as fast as I can. The rain is pouring, but not heavy enough to wash away the memories of sophomore year as my brain keeps on playing it in a loop.

Meeting Autumn at a party. Falling for her. Meeting her parents and seeing the disapproving looks on their faces when they saw my beat-up truck. Realizing that Autumn was a rich girl in a rebellious phase. Having her break up with me because she got back together with her high school boyfriend. Waking up to drunk calls from her. Listening to her apologize about using me as a rebound and telling me that she brought me home to meet the parents because she knew she would get a rise out of her ex. *Fun times.*

I don't even think she remembers making those calls. She wasn't coherent enough and I knew I should have hung up. But there is no undo button in life. She can't take her words back and I can't pretend I didn't listen to her alcohol-fueled confessions.

Sometimes my heart wishes that I could forgive her. It would be so much easier, especially when Andrew died. But Autumn Hargreaves reminds me of the girls who used to take interest in me in high school. The ones who either took interest in me out of pity or because they thought I was someone I wasn't.

Back in my room, I take out my textbooks again and attempt my fucking best at a second round of studying. This is my ticket to a better life. *Maybe I won't feel sorry for myself, then. Maybe I'll find peace. Maybe I'll be happier.*

CHAPTER 9
Gigi

A MONTH LATER

My phone rings for the fourth time. Looking at the caller ID, I exhale a long breath. *Time to face the music, Gigi. The same damn music that's been playing for months.*

"Hey, Mom." I try to sound as unbothered as possible. "What's up?"

"Giuliana Bankowski," she says my name in her *Mom* tone. "Why haven't you been answering my calls and replying to my messages?" *Because I know what you're going to ask me.*

"I've been busy, Mom. Sorry. What do you need?"

I can practically hear the fumes coming out of her ears. "Do I have to need something from my daughter to be in contact with her?"

My heart aches hearing her voice. There was a time when we used to be closer than we are now. It's all my fault. My mother, bless her soul, coddled me after Andrew died. She wouldn't stop calling, wouldn't stop texting. She meant well, I know she did, but at some point I just couldn't handle it anymore.

"No, *Mammina*," I say with a faint smile on my face. "You can call me anytime. I've just been busy. I'm sorry. School has been crazy."

"Thank God for spring break, huh?" *There it is.* "Have you decided on what you're going to do yet?"

Think of happy thoughts, Gigi. Picture the ocean. Picture the park.

My mind betrays me. The brain is a creature of habit. Although I've tried to abandon the last part of my mantra, mental pictures of Andrew play in my head, and this time it's not a good one. It's of him in Marble Crest. At that party. In that house. *Fuck, fuck, fuck. Turn it off.*

I open my eyes, not realizing that I closed them. My visions blurs from unshed tears. *I was doing so well.*

"I, uh, might go to Dad's," I blurt out immediately. "I don't know yet. Or I might stay here." A few of the girls in my dorm wing mentioned staying on campus for the break. Apparently special arrangements can be made. All you have to do is pay a little extra. I might ask them about it.

My mom sighs and hearing it makes me feel guilty. I've changed. She knows it. I know it. I don't know if I can be the old Gigi again. I don't know if she likes the new version of me. I'm quieter, but that's what happens when your boyfriend makes long-term plans with you and then chooses death instead. You change.

"Mom?" I ask when she doesn't say anything.

"I miss you, Giuliana."

"You saw me last month when you came for a visit," I say in a more upbeat tone, trying to cheer her up. "We can meet in the middle if you'd like."

"I want to see you for more than a day trip, honey." She sighs again. "I know it's...hard being back here. But this is your home, Gigi."

I hold back my scream. I want to yell and break things. I

lived in Kinsdale Springs for less than two years, and all of my memorable moments include Andrew—the good ones like when he took me out on our first date or the bad ones like our rough patch. I don't think I can set foot within a one hundred mile radius of that town without exploding into tiny little fragments.

"I'll think about it," is all I manage to say regarding my upcoming spring break plan. "I have to go. My friends are waiting for me. Love you, Mom."

"I love you." Her tone is soft and loving, and listening to her voice makes me wish that I wasn't like this. Scared of Andrew's memories. Scared of the *what-ifs*. I used to be a tough kid once upon a time. *Will I ever become that person again?*

Think of happy thoughts, Gigi.

I examine my face in the mirror. After running a hand through my hair and tidying up the mascara smudge, I close the door to my dorm room and drag myself to lunch.

"Yo, over here!" Zach screams as he waves a hand. Next to him is Zoey, as well his roommate, Kevin.

"Sorry, I'm late," I say, putting my tray down next to Zach's. "Mom called."

"How's Bianca?" Zoey asks in between chews.

"Fine." I guess a one-word answer is not enough for the three of them, because six eyes are watching me take a bite out of my wrap. "She was asking about my spring break plans."

"You need a ride back home, Gigi?" Zach offers, knowing that I don't have a car. There was no point in getting one since everything important in Kinsdale Springs was within walking distance and Andrew was planning to drive me everywhere in college. "Or will you be going with your brother?"

The thought of Lucas Palmer makes me lose my appetite. Or rather, the thought of what he said to me. How dare he accuse me of something that he knows nothing of? Never mind getting to know me, Luke was too busy enjoying his fucking freshman and sophomore years to even hang out with Andrew. And suddenly he wants to act like he had a front-row seat to our relationship? How Becca and Luke are blood-related, I have no clue. She's so cute, and he's the embodiment of a gloomy day, if the gloomy day ingested some downers.

"I might stay here."

The three of them look at one another. It's Zoey who finally says something. "Kai's parents are going to Canada for a month to visit his mom's side of the family. We're planning on staying at their new house for spring break. You want to tag along? His family inherited a farm, and they want to turn it into a bougie version of agritourism or something like that."

"Is Luke going to be there?" I ask, risking a glance to the other corner of the hall where he's sitting, hiding his bad attitude under a baseball cap. The upside of Zoey dating Kai is that she's happy. The downside of it is that Kai is Luke's best friend. Lucky for me, Luke doesn't seem to care much for daylight hangouts, only emerging like Satan himself during nighttime. I can work with that.

"I don't think so," she answers. "He asked about you last week."

"He has my number. He can reach out to me himself." I'm done making an effort with him when all I get is the cold shoulder.

"What happened between you and your stepbrother again?" Zach asks, clueless about the situation.

Now the three of them turn their heads to Luke. "It's amazing how girls in our neighborhood kept pestering me about him when I moved into his house," I say, narrowing my eyes. "When I started school, I realized the issue wasn't zip code specific. Apparently that's his charm—being a jackass. They all said he was mysterious and aloof. I say he's a dick." I can't argue with the fact that he's cute, though, if you're into the dismissive gazes and one-sided conversations that come along with his handsome face.

"Speaking of charming boys and someone asking about you," Zach says with a grin. "I know someone who would be perfect for you." Kevin is shaking his head, laughing. It's common knowledge in our friend group that Zach is hellbent on finding me a husband.

"I'll pass this time, Zach. But thank you."

They say grief comes in waves. If that's true, the conversation with my mom today was like a tide pulling me under. I might have been on a few dates, but after today, after that call, all I can think of is him. My first love.

A sudden pang of anxiety hits me. *Will my love life always be like this? Will I always take one step back every time I think about Andrew?*

CHAPTER 10
Luke

"WELL, I'LL BE DAMNED. THE PRODIGAL SON HAS returned," my father announces with a ghost of a smile, a cigarette dangling between his lips. His steps come nearer as I close the car door.

"Hi, Dad," I reply when he gives me a slight slap on the shoulder.

The shape of the house looks better and better every time I come home, and this time it's no different. It seems like my dad finally got himself a few chairs for the front porch. The paint job doesn't look bad as well; the stucco looks almost as white as the white button-down shirt I have in my duffel bag.

"Bianca is on shift at the hospital," Dad says, his hand turning the doorknob to close the door. "Rebecca has a singing lesson, but Bianca will pick her up on her way home."

"Singing lessons, huh?"

He chuckles, putting a hand on the back of his neck. "She's really good, too. I went to one of the concerts." My dad smiles as he stares at the ground. "Just a bunch of kids. But yeah, your sister can do the falsetto or whatever they call it."

When his eyes finally meet mine, the honey color is tainted with guilt. "It was Bianca's idea. She went to a PTA meeting in my place and the teacher brought it up." When I don't say anything, he continues on the ramble. "We're a two-income household now, Luke. So you know—"

"No, I get it." I make my way to the kitchen, getting myself some water. The whole ride here was fueled by an energy drink. I need something that's not going to give me a heart attack. "It's great for Becca. Happy for her. You don't have to feel bad for providing for your daughter."

"Luke, listen." But then he sighs and decides to cut himself off. "Yeah, she's happy. Bianca has been great with her. Since Gigi doesn't come around anymore, the girls have been bonding. I'm pretty sure they're happier when I'm gone than when I'm here."

A sober and nervous Vincent Palmer is a chatty Vincent Palmer, similar to his drunk persona. Only the talking points are different. Usually I let him go on without saying anything, not wanting to prolong the conversation with either alter ego, but not this time. "Gigi doesn't come around?"

"Gigi hasn't been home since the funeral, son."

I don't know why, but that doesn't sit right with me. When Bianca became a Palmer, I could have sworn that these two wouldn't last long in Kinsdale Springs. Not after having a life in New York. I was waiting for that phone call or message to arrive where Dad would tell me that he was getting a divorce, but the news never came. It wasn't until I started following Gigi's social media a few months after them moving here that I realized why—the New Yorkers turned into townies. Scrolling through her feed and seeing the pictures was like looking at a zebra embracing a life in the aquarium living amongst fishes. But she looked like she was having the time of her life. Why? I have no goddamn clue.

"Luke Palmer! In the flesh!" Ross approaches me, arms open and ready for a man-hug. "Surprised to see you here."

"Well, you invited me," I say with a laugh. "Congratulations on the engagement."

Just as Ross lets go of me, June, his very pregnant fiancée, is pulling me into another hug. The last time I saw her was when we buried Andrew. I smile at the memories of her babysitting me when I was younger, bribing us with bags of candy as long as I wouldn't tell her parents that Ross would come over and the two of them would disappear upstairs. My child mind believed them when they told me they were only listening to music upstairs. They were most definitely fucking. Hopefully, not in my room.

"Congratulations, June."

She squeezes my shoulders and stares me up and down. "You turned into a stunner, Luke."

"I do what I can," I say, smiling.

"Alright, we're going to go greet the other guests. Go mingle."

As June and Ross say hello to the other guests, linked at the arm, I take a look around to observe the familiar faces that are here tonight. I bet Andrew would have loved to be here. He used to beg his parents to drop him off at my place when he knew June was babysitting. The guy had a big crush on her as a kid. He would have loved the self-service bar set up at the corner, too.

I make my way there, fully intending to make myself a rum and Coke. This town is small enough that you can walk home if you're too drunk to drive. My car can stay parked here and I can pick it up tomorrow when it's time for me to go back. I don't want to stay longer than I need to. After breakfast with Becca, I'm out.

I'm pouring myself a drink when I hear a familiar voice greet me. "Hi, Luke."

"Hi, Rachel," I say, putting the Coke bottle in its original place. My head snaps up when I realize who the person is. *Rachel from church.* "How, uh, how are you?"

"Good," she answers. "I don't know if you've heard, but I live with my sister now in Aldenborro."

"I haven't. Good for you. Must be nice to live together."

I have mostly only paid attention to the back of Rachel's head, usually at church. Now that she's in front of me, my mind is going at a hundred miles an hour. Not because I like her, though. Because of something entirely different.

Rachel is slender, blonde, and has blue eyes. Although she's attractive, as far as I know, she was never popular in school. Maybe not at the bottom of the hierarchy, but not at the top of the food chain, either. She and Gigi couldn't be more different. Hell, she and Andrew couldn't be more different. Would he cheat on Gigi with her? It seems like the only thing they had in common was church.

"Rach, can I ask you something?"

"Sure, what is it?" she asks with a smile as she screws the cap of the soda back on.

"Did you sleep with Andrew?" I ask, deciding to just cut right to the chase.

She looks at me in horror. Even under the poor lighting, I can see the color leaving her already pale skin. "Uh, no? Where...where did you hear that from?" She's smiling, but judging by the sound of her voice and the way she can't look me in the eye, I know she's lying.

Fuck.

"Did you?" I don't actually need to hear a verbal confirmation, but fuck me...

"Please don't tell her," she mumbles before hurrying away from me and joining her friends.

Running my hand through my hair, I pull out my phone and do the one thing I know can't wait. Something I should have done weeks ago. I text Gigi.

Are you free tomorrow? We need to talk.

Gigi was telling the truth. And I shat on it. *You're a fucking asshole, Lucas Palmer.*

CHAPTER 11
Gigi

I CAN HEAR THE SOUND OF MY SNEAKERS MEETING the floor as I'm pacing around my dorm room. I wonder why Luke sent that text. When I see the time on my phone, I unlock it and read the chain of texts again to make sure that I'm getting all the details correct.

LUKE

Are you free tomorrow? We need to talk.

I have nothing to say to you, Luke.

I do.

What is it about?

It's better to talk about it in person.

Well, I'm going to the neon party tonight. If you're going, we can talk there.

I'm back home right now. I should be back on campus around noon tomorrow.

Ok.

I'll come by your dorm. 3 pm sounds good?

Cool. See you then.

Someone is knocking on the door and I already know who it is. Sure enough, Luke is standing on the other side when I open it, holding a big Tupperware. I already know what's inside it, too.

"Your mom told me to bring these for you," he says, handing me the orange box.

I should slam the door in his face for the things he accused me of the last time we saw each other, but he did gift me with the thing I've been craving for the longest time—Mom's homemade cannoli.

"Come in."

Luke just stands in the middle of my room, both hands inside his jeans pocket. He looks around, and I realize that this is the first time he's ever been here. His eyes zero in on a framed picture of me and Becca on my desk.

The sound of him clearing his throat makes mine snap back to him. "My dad said you haven't been home in a while."

"Very true," I mumble as I chew on my cannoli. Trying to change the topic, I open the lid to the Tupperware and take out one piece. "Want one?"

"They're for you, Gi." *Why is he speaking to me in a tender tone?*

With my eyes narrowed, I start digging. "Why are you here, Luke? I know it's not just to bring me cannoli." He didn't even want to help me transport my moving boxes, for God's sake.

"I met Rachel."

Think of happy thoughts, Gigi.

"You what?"

"I owe you an apology." For all his growls and scowls, I always appreciated the fact that Luke was a straight shooter. This time is no exception. "I shouldn't have said the things I said to you."

I've never seen this expression on his face before. Luke has never looked at me with such kindness. It lessens the hurt a little bit.

"I forgive you," I say, turning my back to him to put the Tupperware on the desk.

Luke doesn't answer. I hear him shuffling his feet, and I think he's about to leave the room. After all, this is how we communicate, right? In short sentences? I'm about to say goodbye to him when his deep voice whispers out a confession, "I miss him. I miss him but I'm also mad at him. He didn't even leave a fucking note."

My spine goes ramrod straight before I turn around to face him, my jaw slackening. This conversation would have made me sob a few months ago. Now, I just feel the hollowness in my chest. Strangely enough, seeing how Luke looks right now, I also feel like some of the weight has been lifted off my shoulders. Misery loves company.

"I miss him, too," I say with a bitter smile. When Luke doesn't answer, I decide to take my chance and ask the million-dollar question. "Why do you think he did it?"

"I don't know," he admits. "I've been trying to figure it out over and over again. I honestly don't know."

"He was happy by the end, Luke." *Think of happy thoughts, Gigi. Picture the ocean. Picture the park. Picture Andrew in his cap and gown.* "I don't know what Rachel told you, but whatever it was, it wasn't because of that." I feel the pricking behind my eyes. "We worked through all that shit."

"I'm really sorry for being an asshole to you that night. And I'm sorry he cheated on you."

"I'm sorry for stealing your room," I say, trying to lighten the mood. I'm just so done with all of the sadness. So done. Luke actually smirks under his baseball cap. New badge unlocked: something I said is making his permanent frown disappear.

"I'm sorry for being a dick to you when we first met," he says, his mouth still quirking upward. "Well, for always being a dick to you, actually."

"I'm really sorry I accidentally threw away your favorite T-shirt. I thought it was a rag."

"I'm really sorry I told everyone I knew you were a stuck-up princess. In my defense, you call yourself Gigi." Honestly, I get it. The reputation of Gigis everywhere has never been good. It's the name of a chihuahua.

"I'm really sorry I told some girls at school that you might have an STD. In my defense, they were pestering me about you. I think I might have done you a solid there. Not your type." Not that I know what his type is.

I'm half-expecting him to stop this game of apologies and yell at me, but my mouth hangs open when he tilts his head back and starts laughing. "Low blow, Bankowski," he says, his shoulders still moving. "I'm really sorry I told the same thing to a frat guy who asked me about you. I think I even specified it."

Biting my lower lip, I try to swallow down my own giggle. "What do I have?"

"Herpes, of course. I was really drunk, not that it was okay."

"Oh, come on, Luke! You couldn't be more creative? If

you're going to spread gossip, at least make it more original. A rare form or something."

"You're a weird one, Gigi." He gives me a lazy smile "You know that?"

The door to the room bursts open. Kai and Zoey give each other a look when they see us together. They must be shocked that neither of us is holding a knife in our hands, trying to kill the other person. "Uh, hi guys?" Kai sounds amused. "What are you doing here, Luke?"

Luke doesn't take his eyes off me, still grinning wide. I think I hear Zoe ask Kai, "Is Luke smiling? I thought he didn't do that."

"Alright, Gi. I'm heading back," Luke announces as he makes his way out. "See you later, Kai." Looking at my friend, he gives her a nod. "Zoey."

Before I can talk myself out of it, I follow him outside. "Hey, Luke!" I call out once I realize he has ridiculously long legs and I can't match his steps.

"What?" He turns to me and slowly walks backward.

"Friends?"

He turns back around, but I think I see him smile again. "Sure."

CHAPTER 12

Luke

If you had told me three and a half years ago when I first met Gigi that I would be spending a whole week with her, I would have told you to kiss my ass. Yet here I am, packing a bag full of booze and her suitcase in my truck, getting ready to leave for Kai's house in the middle of nowhere.

"Zach, Pierre, and Lola all have food poisoning," Zoey announces while grimacing, her phone still clutched in her hand. "Must have been from the takeout place they went to last night. Guess it's just the four of us."

"And on spring break, too. That's rough." Gigi pulls out her own and a second later, three notification sounds ring. It's for our group chat—Party in the Barnhouse.

GIGI

Get well soon, you three. Text us if you need anything. You will be missed :(

Although the iceberg between Gigi and I has melted, I wouldn't say we've bonded. At least not enough that this trip won't be awkward. Sure, we don't avoid one another anymore and say hi when we bump into each other on campus or at parties, but a week? Kai and Zoey are dating. I'm not a moron. They'll be all over one another once we get there. What am I going to do with her? My introverted ass is already dreading spending seven whole days with her extroverted ass.

It's too fucking late to cancel now.

I breathe out a peaceful exhale when the three of them start dozing off thirty minutes into the drive. Almost three years in college and I'm still not used to this. Having a steady group of friends. Going on trips with them. Partying. Bonding.

Most people had a trial run in high school. My experience was a whole fucking lot different. Aside from hanging out with Andrew, my life consisted of making sure I had good enough grades to make it out of Kinsdale Springs and Becca was taken care of. *And that Dad wasn't dead somewhere.*

People didn't want to hang out with me, anyway. After everything that happened to our family, when there were only two Palmer boys left standing, everyone gravitated toward Andrew. They were right to do so. He was the beacon of hope with his charm and smile, somewhat untouched by tragedy. I was the more damaged one. The angry one. The rude one. The one who caused everything to fall apart.

It's been six months since he left and never came back, and sometimes I still can't believe that I'm still here and he isn't. If anyone had placed a bet on which one of us would break first, I'm sure they would have picked me.

From the rearview mirror, I see Gigi stretching her arms and Zoey on her phone. They must have woken up when my mind was focused on Andrew. I wonder if Gigi remembers that the six-month mark was two days ago.

"Are you bummed that Pierre is sick?" Zoey asks her in a soft, sleepy voice.

Gigi smiles as she shakes her head. "I feel bad for him, though. Zach hyped up the trip so bad. I'm pretty sure Pierre bought a cowboy hat."

"Does he know that this is not that kind of farm?" Zoey asks, giggling. "Does he know Zach's parents are renovating the place to turn it into a farm stay for tourists with a petting zoo and a knock-off Starbucks?"

The girls start laughing loudly. I tune them out when Zoey starts talking about how hot Pierre is and how perfect he is for Gigi. I'm not used to this, either. Listening to women snicker about men. One of these days, I will probably thank Kai for taking me under his wing during freshman year and forcing me out of my shell, but today is not the day. Especially not when I hear the words *dick size* and *let's guess* from the back.

"We're here," I say, unbuckling my seatbelt. "Home sweet home, Kai. Wake up, man." Kai yawns, but he doesn't say anything, only staring at the barn that belongs to the property. We all look at him as he stays still like a statue, still silent.

"Babe, seriously, wake up," Zoey says, nudging his shoulder. "We have to get the keys to the house from the day workers. Your mom said they only work until five. It's already four-fifty."

Only when Kai answers do I realize how pale he looks. "I don't feel so good."

It's too fucking late to cancel now.

"Like you're sick?" Zoey asks. "Like food poisoning, sick?"

"I don't think they got food poisoning from the takeout place," is all he says. He's about to say something else, but has the good grace to stop himself and jump out of the car. The three of us gawk at him when he starts pouring the contents of his guts out on the gravel road.

"Fuck," Gigi mutters under her breath.

Kai cleans himself up before going with Zoey to the staff

lounge to meet with one of the employees. Gigi just got off the phone with her mom when I speak. "You want to go to Kinsdale Springs instead? We can pick them up before classes start."

"It's the other way."

"It's doable." I shrug. He is important to me and I'm not excited about the idea of spending spring break at home, either, but the thought of sharing a toilet bowl with Malakai is causing me to shudder. It's a shit situation, literally.

"It's already late."

"We can go tomorrow morning if you want."

"I don't want to go back," she whispers. "I'd rather stay here."

I'm about to protest, but then I notice her biting her bottom lip like she's about to cry. I nod, understanding. She doesn't need to say anything else. *She remembers.* I feel lines forming on my forehead looking at her. My heartstrings tug.

Giuliana Bankowski crying is not something you want to see on a daily basis, because when someone usually walks around as happy and bubbly as she does, the sight of her right now is heartbreaking.

Pulling her closer by wrapping my arms around her shoulders, I surprise even myself with the gentleness of my tone. "Then we're staying."

CHAPTER 13

Luke

TWELVE YEARS OLD

HUFFING OUT A HARSH BREATH, I SHOVE MY baseball cleats into my duffel bag. Mom is leaning on the door jamb with coffee in one hand and guilt in her eyes. Dad can't help it that he's out of town, but she's right here.

"Please try to understand, Luke." She approaches me and takes a seat on the bed. "I would love to if I could, but we have a really important seminar at work today."

"I understand." As much as I want her to come to my baseball game, I turn twelve today. I'm old enough to understand that with my sister being born a year ago, my parents would need to work more. Earn extra money.

"I told your uncle to record a video," she says with a small smile. "We can watch it together tonight."

"Does Becca really have to come with us?" I complain. That little crybaby has been infiltrating every corner of my life. *I hate her!* I loved being an only child.

"Well who's going to watch her otherwise, silly?" I must look upset, because Mom curls her arms around me and gives me a kiss on the head. "I know it has been an adjustment, Luke, but your sister is still so tiny. She needs a lot of love from us." She kisses me again before looking at me in the eye. "All of us. Also you." Her index finger boops my nose. "You're her favorite, you know."

"I know," I groan, rolling my eyes.

My mom's fingers run through my curls. She stops the brushing and runs through the length of the strands instead, narrowing her eyes as she does it. "I need to trim your hair again. It's getting too long."

I want to ask her to take me to the hairdresser instead. I want to tell her that my friends don't get their haircuts from their moms anymore, but I know it costs money, so I just stay quiet.

"Let's go down," she says. "Andrew and his family will be here any minute now. Plus, I still need to get the milk for your sister ready."

My bad mood disappears at the mention of Andrew. Even though he's only ten, he's my best friend.

My mom says God isn't real and my grandma from Dad's side doesn't like that, so every Sunday, she always takes me to her church. Mom told Dad to make her stop, but he says there's no harm in me going. I don't mind. Not only do I get to meet most of the family from my dad's side, I also get to spend time with Andrew. We play sports now—me baseball and him basketball—and sometimes we go to each other's games. Lucky me, today is Saturday. An extra day with Andrew! I know it's only because somebody needs to drive me to the field and his parents offered to do it, but how cool is this?

"Happy birthday, Luke!" Andrew yells, shoving a big blue paper bag toward me. "It's Monopoly!"

"Thanks, Andrew." I grin as I snatch the bag away from him, widening my eyes when I spot 'The Simpsons' Edition' written on the box. I look at the two adults standing behind him. "Thanks, Auntie Judith. Thanks, Uncle Mike."

Coach gives me a hug before telling me to go over to my teammates. They're waiting for me by the bleachers. When I run up to them, they start singing Happy Birthday to me. Most of their hands are sticky from the orange slices and the muffins, but I shake it, anyway. It's my birthday and we just won the game. I feel so happy! Uncle Mike said he got it on video when I scored the home run. I can't wait to show my parents. Nothing can ruin my mood, not even disgusting fingers.

"Can you take Becca for a second?" Auntie Judith asks. "My phone has been ringing this whole time."

I take my sister in my arms, pinching her chubby cheek. "Do you like coming to my game, Becca?" She just coos and giggles. Don't tell anybody, but even if she's annoying, she is the cutest thing I have ever seen in my life.

A few boys from my team are trying to get Becca to do some tricks when my aunt and uncle jog toward us. I frown when I see how panicked they seem. Andrew and I give each other looks before facing them again.

"We need to go, guys," Uncle Mike says in between heavy breaths.

"Why?" Andrew asks. "We promised one of Luke's teammates we would wait until his mom comes. She's stuck in traffic."

"I'll ask another parent to wait with him," Auntie Judith says to my uncle before walking over to Russel's mom.

"Luke." Uncle Mike doesn't look happy and it's making me feel weird. I feel like my heart is beating really fast right now and I don't know if it's normal or not. "Something bad happened at church, buddy." His eyes look glassy as he bends down to my level and holds onto my shoulders.

"There was a fire and your mom...your mom and the others...they were trapped."

"My mom is at work," I answer immediately. "And she doesn't believe in Jesus." What is Uncle Mike talking about? It must be someone else's mom.

"Lu—" he tries to say my name again, but clams up and looks at the field instead. When he looks back at me, Uncle Mike seems weird. "Son, your mom and the others were at church. They wanted to throw you a surprise party. Your grandma rented out the rec center. She invited all your cousins and your other grandparents." He breathes out a long breath, shaking his head. "We were supposed to be here with you while they set everything up."

"Is my dad also there?"

Uncle Mike shakes his head. "He really is out of town for work. I already called him. He's on his way back."

"Are they okay?" My uncle looks at me. I've never seen him like this before. His lips are trembling. Auntie Judith is now standing next to him, her eyes equally sad as Uncle Mike's. "Uncle Mike, are they okay?"

He slowly shakes his head. "I'm sorry, Luke. I'm so sorry," he finally answers. He has one of his hands on his hips and the other one over his eyes. "None of them made it out."

"No," I whisper. My mom doesn't think God is real. Grandma and the other Palmers always go to church on Sundays. I think this is a lie, but the other parents here are all whispering around me. They're all saying that it happened. Someone behind me mentions that my cousins came with their moms and dads to the rec center.

Auntie Judith is reaching for Becca, but I take a step back, and then another, and then another.

She needs a lot of love from us.

I hold her tight in my arms, my palm protecting the back of her neck just like Mom showed me. If this is true, who's going to love Becca now when Dad is away working? I lean in close to her ear and whisper, "I'm not going to hate you anymore. You need a lot of love, Becca."

CHAPTER 14

Gigi

"You need to stay at least five feet away from us, man," Luke says to Kai. I think he's joking, but with him? Who knows. I'm with him on this one, though. Kai looks like he's about to projectile vomit for the second time.

"We're going to quarantine ourselves in my parents' bedroom," Kai replies, pausing himself every few seconds to probably swallow the puke that's about to come up. "If I have it, Zoe's probably going to be sick soon, too. You guys can have the rooms upstairs. There's an adjoining bathroom for the two of you. We figured you probably don't want to be sharing a toilet bowl with us."

Never have I ever been more grateful to stay in my dorm room last night doing a cleaning session instead of going out with my friends.

"You need anything?" Luke asks.

"Is your fridge stocked up?" I ask Kai. "I can make you soup or something."

"Thanks, Gigi." Kai gives me a weak smile. "Our day staff, Molly, is picking dinner up for all of us from the restaurant next door and some medicine. If you two need anything, you can make a list and give it to her later. She said she'd show you both the land tomorrow. A lot of things are still under renovation, but the animals are here and the indoor pool is already working."

"And the booze," Zoey adds. "Don't *not* have fun on our account."

Kai motions with his hands for us to follow him. "I'll show you to your rooms."

Holding onto the banister, I follow the other three up the stairs. My jaw almost drops to the floor when Luke grabs the handle of my suitcase and carries it for me. Until now, I've never spent longer than a few hours with him. I didn't know that Luke Palmer was such a gentleman. I guess the saying *it's always the ones you don't expect* doesn't only apply to criminals.

"We got it, Kai," I tell him, quickly pulling my hand away when I realize that I'm touching his forearm. I grimace when I remember that he used the sleeve to wipe his mouth before. "You go get some rest." Trying to make out the fate of my best friend, I give her a quick once-over. "If you're feeling up for it, you can always chill with us, Zo."

"We'll see about tomorrow," she says. "I have to take care of this big baby first."

"We got a whole week here," Kai says. "I'm pretty sure whatever fucking bug this is will be out of my system in a few days. I'm going to show you guys a good time, I promise."

I'm about to knock on the open door when I see Luke sprawled on the bed. His honey eyes light up, turning into a shade of gold, listening to Becca tell him about the sleepover she's invited to on the weekend. Ever since we've agreed on a truce, this guy has been full of surprises. I know he loves Becca to death, but with him only going back during school breaks, I thought he was too busy, doing stupid shit boys do when they go to college, to keep up with their bond. I didn't know the two of them video chat and he looks this happy when they do.

Not wanting to seem like a creep, I clear my throat. "Dinner's here."

He turns his head around and nods. When Becca notices me lurking in the background, I hear the loud, playful sound of her voice. "You didn't tell me Gigi was with you! Don't kill her, Luke."

Luke is on his feet, about to stand up. At Becca's words, he smiles. A big, toothy one that goes from one ear to the other. Much like Andrew's, it's beautiful. And all the way down to the dining room, he still lights up, his face basking in happiness.

"Do you miss her?" I ask, trying to make small talk in between blowing the cream of mushroom soup on my spoon.

"Sometimes." I'm about to give up on my attempt to have a conversation, since it seems like I'm getting the quiet version of Luke tonight, but then he surprises me. "Ever since Uncle Mike gave her his old tablet, she's been video chatting me all the time. Hard to miss someone when you talk to them almost every day."

"You don't miss being with her?" I cock an eyebrow. "Like in the same room?"

He stops eating, pinning me down with his eyes instead. "Already got a lifetime's worth of being in the same room as her." *What the hell is that supposed to mean?*

"How's your studies going?" I ask again, not being able to resist. We might be spending more time now that Zoey is dating Kai, but it's always in a group setting. I can't help but want to know more about the elusive stepbrother who never once bothered to meet me halfway on the one Christmas and one Easter that I spent with my mom instead of in New York. He was always only there for a day before leaving for Andrew's house and then to Kai's hometown. I always got the impression that it was because of me.

"It's good. Lots of work this year, but everything is fine."

"You're going to be a senior next year. What are you going to do after you graduate?"

Luke raises an eyebrow. "You're asking a lot of questions, Gi. I know for sure my dad didn't put you up to this. What's with the interrogation?"

"Oh, please." I roll my eyes. "It was only five at max." When he still has an amused look on his face, I let out a sigh. "You know, our parents have been married for three years now, and I still know the bare minimum about you."

"I still know the bare minimum about *you*." Luke shrugs. "You don't see me complaining about it."

The only thing I know about Luke, the only thing people talk about, is the horrible thing that happened when the church burned down in Marble Crest. This is why I give Luke a pass for being an ice prince. No wonder girls dig him. He's a perfect ten, if you're into I-can-fix-him vibes. How Andrew was still sunshine and rainbows after losing all of his cousins and most of the generation above them, leaving only him, Luke, and Becca to carry on the Palmer last name, I have no idea. Maybe that's why he killed himself.

I hate that my mind wanders off to Andrew, so I do something to reroute my night. "What do you say to drinking one of those wines that Zoey brought? We can play a round of rapid-fire questions? I lived in your room, Luke. It's weird that we know next to nothing about each other."

"Fine."

"Really?" I ask, double-checking. I was so sure he was going to say no.

He shrugs. "With the two of them fighting off the fucking plague, what else are we going to do tonight?"

CHAPTER 15
Luke

THE TWO OF US SIT ON OPPOSITE ENDS OF A VERY long, very expensive-looking couch; a luxury that we never had in my childhood home in Kinsdale Springs. When we moved in there from Marble Crest after Mom died, Dad got us a two-seater from Craigslist. Becca was a baby by then, and with him being gone a lot, it was mostly just me using it. When Dad started looking for happiness at the bottom of liquor bottles, he got himself a rocking chair for the living room. Who knows? Maybe alcohol hits better when you're swaying back and forth at eleven at night in the dark.

I wonder if the girl swirling her wine around in her glass here with me knows that her stepdad was an alcoholic. I can't imagine him putting that on the bio of whatever online dating profile he created.

"This wine tastes like shit." Gigi's voice echoes in the living room of the farmhouse.

"Boxed wine not up to your standard, princess?"

"Whatever," she says, rolling her eyes that are glued to her screen. "Anyway, I found a good list of questions online." Gigi closes the distance between us, scooting over and handing me her phone. "I'll go first. Easy. Midnight owl or early riser?"

"Midnight owl," I answer without hesitation. "I like to sleep in." My finger accidentally clicks on the arrow at the bottom, and I feel my lips twitching into a smile when I see Gigi put 'questions for breaking the ice with someone who's quiet' into the search bar. Ever since Kai and Zoey became official and our group of friends merged into one, I've been realizing more and more that I might have misjudged this girl when we first met. Her niceness is actually not a façade; she's actually pretty cool. "I got one. Would you rather be able to shapeshift or teleport?"

"Hmmm." She taps her chin with her finger like she's taking this seriously. She probably fucking is. "Teleport. Tickets to New York are expensive as hell."

"How much do they go for?" I ask.

"Around four hundred bucks during the high season. I had to cut my budget for presents way down when I went last Christmas."

"Do the ticket prices change?" I blurt out before I can stop myself.

Gigi looks at me with an amused look, her head slightly tilted. "Of course?"

My face is all heat right now. "I...I've never been on a plane before," I admit in a low voice. I've never even crossed state lines.

I'm mentally getting ready for Gigi to make fun of me, but she says nothing. She doesn't even fucking flinch to what I said. Gigi just grabs the phone from me and smiles, saving me from further embarrassment. "My turn. Milk first or cereal first?"

"Neither," I say, grinning. "I don't like milk. It tastes like soaked cardboard." When she just shakes her head, I grab the phone from her and try to pick a more interesting question.

The alcohol must already be working, because she's laughing so hard when the one I'm asking isn't even all that funny. "The longest time you've vegged out on a couch watching TV?"

"Latchkey kid here," she says, raising her hand like she's in school. "The TV was basically my nanny. I spent most of my evenings and weekends glued to the screen."

Not the New York life I've pictured her having. "Was it lonely? Being an only child?"

She nods. "That's why I was so happy when Mom said she was going to marry your dad. I knew you were going to leave for college when they announced their engagement, but I always wanted to have a little sister. Becca doesn't disappoint. She's the best."

We continue on with our stupid interview, but my mind can't shake what Gigi said. How she feels about Becca. I've never seen Gigi as my sister, but the fact that she was there for mine makes me feel...happy? Thankful? *The wine must be getting to me as well.*

I don't know when it started, but the stakes of the questioning got higher. We moved on from harmless ones to shit like *when was the first time you fell in love* and *what is your biggest life goal.* The booze is up a notch as well, considering the fact we're on our second shot of vodka.

"You ready?" she asks, her phone in her hand. "Do you believe in heaven?" Her face pales when she realizes what she just asked me. "So...sorry, Luke. I'll look for another one."

"It's fine," I answer with a smile to reassure her. "I'd like to think that there's a Heaven somewhere. If Heaven looks anything like Earth, Marble Crest must be filled with Palmers." Maybe I'm drunker than fuck right now, or maybe it's the way she doesn't look at me with pity, but the thought of all of my dead family members doesn't hurt me tonight. "What about you?" I ask.

"If there is one..." she slurs her words just like I'm slurring mine. "I think Andrew is laughing his head off looking at us right now. Being friends." She's not wrong. He probably would.

I don't answer that, but I do groan when I see her pouring us another glass of wine for us. "Gi, fuck. You're drinking me under the table," I say, rubbing my eyes. By now, both of us are slouched on the floor like rugs, using the couch as a backrest.

"You're a late bloomer, Luke Palmer." She shrugs, bringing her glass closer to her lips as she hands me mine.

"You're using my confession against me." I can't help the grin that breaks out on my face. Before we started drinking vodka out of coffee mugs, I told her the first time I properly started drinking for fun was when I was a college freshman. When Kai took me to my first house party, I made a mental note to stop the moment I graduated, swearing to myself that I'd never binge drink like my dad after I stepped into the real adult world.

"I am not!" Gigi squeals. "It's just what it is, Luke. Nobody gets a trophy for having a high alcohol tolerance, anyway." *Tell that to my dad*. "I have to pee."

Gigi stands up, only to wobble back down again. She falls on me, both of our bodies creating a plus sign with her head facing down. Her eyes widen in horror when she sees that my hoodie is all purple, courtesy of my wine that just spilled. Her eyes immediately scan the room, probably to look for a tissue.

"Let's call it a night, yeah? I think you've had enough."

"Shit, I'm really sorry, Luke."

Gigi looks like she's in panic mode as she frantically tries to rub the stain with the sleeve of her shirt. I grab her hand in mine so that she'd stop. "Gi, all good. Promise," I say. "Just go pee and get yourself ready for bed. I'll clean up."

The girl doesn't move, though. She's still sitting on my lap with her palms on my chest and her dark hair all wild. My fingers, having a mind of their own, tuck the loose strands of her hair behind her ear. Both of our bodies stiffen after that. Her gray eyes snap up to meet mine, and I'm not sure what they're trying to fucking tell me. I swallow the lump in my throat when I realize how close we are at this second. One small move forward and our noses would be touching.

The questions...the way Gigi's body was on me...the way she made me laugh...I shouldn't be having these feelings for her. *For a lot of fucking reasons.* How did she go from being someone I only meet two days a year at most to a girl who I'm going to spend the whole week with? This would be the perfect setup for a hookup, except she's off-limits. The most off-limits there can be.

CHAPTER 16
Gigi

I don't know what's happening to me. Liquid courage? Six long months of not being touched? A mental breakdown? But right now, the only thing I can focus on is the way I shudder the moment Luke's fingertips graze my earlobe. Is this the most pathetic reason for being turned on? Yes. Is the alcohol making me not care? Also yes. The alcohol is, in fact, making me not care about a lot of things concerning Lucas Palmer.

I gently place one hand on his cheek, and before I know it, my lips are planted on his lips. My heart beats faster when Luke kisses me back. Soft and gentle, two things I don't associate with him. When he straightens his back and repositions himself, my hands create a loop around his neck, fusing our bodies together even more.

Luke's tongue tastes a little bit like cheap vodka and boxed wine, and a lot like something I will regret in the morning.

"Gigi." My name comes out with a breath as he breaks the kiss, bringing our foreheads together instead. "What are you doing?"

I wish I knew the answer to that question. All I know is

that he is the only person that I have been interested in touching ever since...*Don't think about it, Gigi.*

Think of happy thoughts, Gigi. Picture the ocean. Picture the park. Picture...Shut up. Shut up. Shut up.

I don't say anything back, diving back into him instead, melting our mouths together in a twisted union. Taking his baseball cap off, I focus on the sensation of raking my fingers over his dirty blond curls. They're hanging above his ears now. When I moved to Kinsdale Springs, Luke had a buzz cut. He was just a few months younger than I am today, but he looked so different. He looked like a boy. I wonder if Luke thinks I'm juvenile right now. Like I'm an immature drunk who wants to jump the guy she's left alone with. He wouldn't be wrong to think that, though. I'm shamelessly dry humping him while our friends are upstairs.

Luke moves his mouth to my neck before pushing my hair to one side and leaving trails of kisses on my collarbone. I can't bring myself to be ashamed of my A-cup tits when one of his big hands reaches under my wool sweater. The moan that comes out of me when he rolls his thumb over my nipple is a testament to that.

I shouldn't want this. I shouldn't be doing this. I should stop and say goodnight. But fuck it, I'm only human. And when Luke grips my hips, forcing me to slow down my movement, my clit feels like it's being robbed of the friction.

"We should stop. You're drunk," he says while still flicking my nipple and trailing his lips on my shoulder, making no sign that he's going to listen to his own advice. If that's the rationale he is using, it's weak as hell. He acts like I don't feel the bulge that's straining his jeans.

"I'm not too drunk that I can't consent."

"Fuck," he groans. He pinches the bridge of his nose, closing his eyes. "You shouldn't have said that."

"One-time thing." I gasp when he grabs the curve of my ass. "What about you? Are you too drunk for this?"

Luke breaks our contact. When he gently puts me down on the floor and stands up, I'm mentally preparing for him to go back to his guarded self and accuse me of being insane. Instead, he holds out his hand for me to take. "Sober enough to know what I'm doing, but drunk enough that I don't care as much as I probably fucking should." I grab his hand and he smirks, immediately letting it go to loop his arm around my shoulder. He lowers his lips to my ears and whispers, "Let's go upstairs. I don't think you'd want our friends to know that you're about to hook up with your stepbrother."

My heart is racing the whole time we make our way to the second floor. By the time we're in Kai's room, the poor thing is about to explode. I know Luke smokes pot at parties sometimes; I wonder if he brought any with him. I could really use it right about now.

The first thing I do once the back of my knees reach the edge of Malakai's full mattress is pull Luke's hoodie over his head. Something like guilt washes over me when I spot the tattoo on one of his pecs. In New York, I went to a Catholic school long enough to know who that is. *Andrew the Apostle.*

Luke follows where my eyes are going and swallows. He hovers over me when I take a seat on the bed, his thumb caressing my cheek. "Gi, we don't have to do this," he says in a gentle tone I have only heard a handful of times from him, and only once directed at me. *During that night.*

"I want to, Luke," I whisper. "Make me forget. You know what this week is." *The six-month mark of a wasted death.*

Although he stiffens, pausing momentarily, that seems to do it for him. He nods before planting his lips on mine again, even slower and more thoughtful than before. He breaks the kiss for a moment to look at me, scanning my face as if to make sure I'm okay, and I appreciate that he's doing this for me.

We're not that close, but he must sense what a big step this is for me, regardless of the fact that I'm choosing to be with him.

I don't know who undresses who first, but before I finish with my self-calming mantra, both of us are lying naked. Luke lowers his head, gripping the sides of my thighs with his big hands. Once my drunken mind realizes what he's about to do, I lean on my elbows.

"I don't want that, Luke. I want you inside me."

He cocks an eyebrow as if that's the most ridiculous thing on Earth. "You sure?" I nod, earning a chuckle from him. "Can't say I've heard that one before. Suit yourself," he says.

He straightens his back and kneels between my legs, rubbing his length a few times before aligning his dick with my opening. His bulge is veiny, with a little curve at the circumcised tip. I feel my face heating up and my chest thundering at the pressure of his penis going inside. *It's happening. Luke is going inside me. I'm going to fuck Luke.*

I wince at the way he's stretching me, holding onto his shoulders for support. Moral support? Emotional support? There's too much going on in my mind and in this room to analyze my feelings and color-code it.

"Luke," I whimper.

"Gigi, fuck, you're so tight."

He pulls himself out of me completely before going back in. After a few thrusts, the discomfort has worn off and something else takes its place. With every plunge inside, I feel more vibrations in my core. When I wrap my legs around Luke's hips, he groans out my name as he goes deeper inside me.

As his thumb draws circles on my clit, I completely forget why us doing this is frowned upon. Just like everything else that Luke has been doing, the way he's getting me off would cause my jaw to drop on the floor with how gentle it is if I wasn't already using my mouth to pant. *Is this what sex is supposed to feel like?*

I feel the burn in the lower part of my body and I don't know what's coming. Judging by the way Luke picks up the pace, he's not far off from his own climax. Just as I am about to tell him to slow down because it hurts and go back to being gentle again, he finishes, shooting a ribbon of warm liquid inside me.

"Sorry." He chuckles into the crook of my neck. "You felt so good I couldn't hold off anymore." Luke kisses the crown of my head before trailing his lips down my stomach. "I'll make it up to you, right now, Gi."

"What are you waiting for?" I ask, breathing heavily when he stops giving me pecks that send tingles under my skin. "I thought you were going to make it up to me?" When I look down, I see Luke staring at me. His eyes are narrowed and his jaw is tight. "What's wrong?" I ask, still spread out on my back.

He stands up and goes to the bathroom, only to come back with a towel. As he wipes me clean, Luke finally speaks. "You didn't tell me you were a virgin," he says through gritted teeth.

CHAPTER 17

Luke

YOU STUPID IDIOT.

You banged your stepsister.

You banged your dead cousin's girlfriend.

You popped her cherry.

I wish there was a handbook for this. How does one exactly deal with the aftermath of something so fucked up, you might ask? I've got zero clue. I'll let you know once I stop staring at Kai's blood-soaked blanket.

Andrew was hunting her down ever since he laid eyes on her that November his junior year. They were dating the whole of senior year. How the fuck is she still a virgin?

I didn't think it was possible, but a new sense of dread pops up. An even bigger one. *You're just making bad decision after bad decision tonight, Luke*

"We didn't use a condom," I say, pinching the bridge of my nose while closing my eyes. On a scale of one to ten, this is an eleven on stupidity.

"I'm on the shot."

"Huh?" My head is too busy thinking about how I'm

going to explain knocking Gigi up to our family that I don't register what she's saying.

"I'm on the shot," she repeats herself. "Like the flu shot, but for babies. The birth control shot."

Relief washes over me, making the stream of cold sweat oozing out of my pores stop. Not by a lot, but enough. "Gi, how the fuck are you still a virgin?" I ask, deciding to just get on with it. "You never...You didn't..."

"No, I didn't sleep with Andrew; if that's what you're asking."

Still lying down, she looks at the ceiling. Drowning in her silence, I know that she's thinking about something. Maybe about the past, maybe she's regretting sleeping with me. Whatever it is, I feel my heart soften for her. I shouldn't. I should probably head to the other room and pretend like this never happened, but holy hell. I just used a virgin like she was some fucking cum dumpster. She didn't even get off. Her last boyfriend died less than a year ago. I'll be damned if I don't comfort her right now. Pillow talk is the least I could do. Besides, it's not like I can un-fuck Gigi.

Resting my head on my arm, I lay down next to her. My gaze is also on the ceiling when I ask, "Why?"

"It just never happened." She shrugs, trying to make it seem like it doesn't affect her, but Gigi sounds sad.

"Was it because of what happened with Rachel?"

"Maybe."

"What happened?" I had this idea in my head of what their relationship was like. I thought the two of them were happy. Normal. At least that's what I always thought every time I saw them pop up on my social media feed.

Normal people don't cheat on their girlfriends. Normal people don't kill themselves. Normal people don't lose their virginities to their stepbrothers. I swallow down my disappointment in myself. *Normal stepbrothers don't sleep with their stepsisters, either.*

"Well, if you must know..." She sighs, and when I steal a glance to watch her face, I catch her closing her eyes. "We were waiting until graduation. It was supposed to be a graduation present for the both of us. Then the whole Rachel thing happened and we went through a rough patch. By the time we were back to how we were, it was orientation week. You know what happened a few weeks after that. So...yeah. Never got around to it, I guess." *Don't I fucking know it.*

I'm about to tell her that what she did was stupid and she should have told me, but Gigi looks so broken next to me. A part of me knows this is wrong, so wrong that I want to sucker punch myself, but I turn to face her and my lips rest on her forehead. When her arm drapes around my waist, I don't stop her. I don't even flinch, letting myself enjoy the warmth of her body instead.

"Don't offer someone a one-time thing and then let them have sex with you bareback ever again. I know I'm clean but not all guys get tested regularly. And you have to go to the bathroom, Gi. You need to pee, otherwise you might get an infection."

We both laugh. Why did I decide that giving her an impromptu sex education would make this situation less awkward? I have no fucking idea. No handbook. I'm treading in the dark here. Pitch black. This is the best I can do, sue me.

"Soon." She smiles, and I hate that the sight of her makes me do the same. "Let's just be here for a minute."

"Hey, Gi, can I ask you something?"

"Are you going to ask me why I slept with you?"

"Yeah."

"Alcohol, boredom, and I just don't care anymore."

I cock an eyebrow. "You don't care anymore?"

"I mean..." She pauses with a shrug. "I treated my V-card

like it was some special, magnificent thing. Like it was a gift to the world. Clearly, it's not. Andrew apparently didn't care about his and everyone in college is screwing like rabbits. Why should I miss out on having fun?"

Knowing Gigi and how she is, she's going to regret saying all this shit tomorrow once she's sober. *I wonder if she's going to regret me.*

"What we did, Gi..." I curse at myself in my head. "That's not how you're supposed to have sex for the first time. I hope you know that." Fucking hell, even my first time was more special than this. *Amy Charmichaels. Pizza date. Lots of foreplay and definitely with a condom on. And not with someone who was double forbidden.*

"It was fine, Luke." She pulls me in closer as if she wants to reassure me that it was the right decision. "I had friends who lost their virginities in the backseat of some Tinder date's car. Some of them lost it in the locker room. I mean...Andrew lost his at a house party in a bathroom. This was nice."

"How do you know that?" *Andrew fucked for the first time in a bathroom? I thought he would be a candles and petals kind of guy.*

"Andrew?"

I nod.

"Someone sent me a video."

CHAPTER 18
Gigi

EIGHTEEN YEARS OLD

I SWALLOW A BIG GULP OF NOTHING WHEN MY EYES catch the three big circles on my calendar. 18th of May, 25th of May, and 30th of June—all marked by a red Sharpie.

When we decided on what to do, it was before Christmas. Graduation still felt like a long time away back then, but now? Andrew's is three months and eighteen days from today, and after mine takes place, we're finally going to do it. We're finally going to have sex.

I'm pacing around the room, taking a mental note of everything that we said we would prepare. Andrew still needs to buy the condoms, and I went to the gynecologist yesterday to inform myself about the Depo-Provera injection. He still needs to buy his ticket to New York, and I still need to lie to my dad and tell him that I will be arriving a day later than I actually am. We still need to book a room for the night.

This is finally happening, Gigi. You're going to have sex. And Andrew is going to join you to go to New York and meet your dad for the first time.

The phrases *purity ring* and *son of a preacher man* pop up every time his school friends meet me and ask why we haven't done the deed yet. I can't blame them. He's the only guy on his basketball team who hasn't, and I quote, *dipped his dick in pussy* yet.

But the decision to abstain from sex didn't come from his religious background, even if most people seem to think so and have no qualms about using the Palmers' devout Christianity as a running joke. No, it's coming from me. My wonderful boyfriend is just too nice to say anything back. I wouldn't care if he told them the truth, it's not like I go to school with these idiots, anyway. I only have to see them during Andrew's games and the occasional parties.

Andrew is your normal teenage boy. When we both got ourselves out of the friendzone, he came in hot and heavy. And it's not like we don't do anything at all. I know what a dick tastes like on my tongue and what a tongue feels like on my vagina. It's just the dick in vagina part that I have hang-ups about.

But he knows why I don't want to rush into it. When I told him that my parents had me young, and seeing their marriage practically disintegrate in front of my eyes because of a lethal combination of crazy work schedules, high living costs, and having a kid make me scared shitless about having an unplanned pregnancy, he has been nothing but understanding. Even when I told him that I was waiting because I wanted to make sure that it's with the right person. The dude must be an actual saint because if he was offended by what I said, he didn't show it.

I was a surprise baby from my parents' one night stand. They got married soon after the second stripe on the pregnancy test showed up because they were raised Catholic and it was the right thing to do.

It turns out you can still do everything right and still make a mess of yourself.

They used protection? My mom still got knocked up. They got married? The two of them still got divorced. So when my parents decided to do the birds and bees talk with me and told me to make sure that whoever I have sex with is the right guy, I took that shit to heart. They know first-hand what would happen if you do it with the wrong person.

Is Andrew the right guy? I blush at the thought. I'm 99 percent sure. He's cute, sweet, and charming. He also brings me flowers every time he watches me cheer, even though it's for Kinsdale Springs High and the sport I'm cheering for is football. I'm planning on saying I love you soon, if he doesn't beat me to it, of course.

It blows my mind that he and Luke could be as close as they are. I haven't met him enough times to be able to form a solid opinion about him, but the whispers I hear at school? God damn...people say he was one of the rudest, most arrogant guys to have ever roamed the halls. He rejects invites to parties and never goes to dances like he's too cool for school. Apparently, he also sleeps with girls only to distance himself from them afterward. I know this from one of his victims. She's in my bio class. When she figured out who I was, she couldn't keep her mouth shut about him. Luke should know better. The more you ghost them, the more interested they become.

❧

My bladder is begging me to wake up. Cursing at myself for chugging down the cup of tea I had before bed, I slowly open my eyes. I'm summoning the willpower to actually stand up and drag myself to the toilet when I hear the sound of someone's car engine downstairs. Mom must be back from her shift.

I wonder what time it is right now. My phone is in my hands, but my brain blurs out the information I was looking for just five seconds ago. Instead, my eyes zone in on the notification that pops up.

I click.

UNKNOWN NUMBER

Do you think church boy will confess his sins?

Under the text is a thumbnail of a video. Without pressing the triangle in the middle, I already have a hunch about what I'm going to see. The thumbnail shows a guy with dirty blond locks that I sometimes twirl with my index finger grabbing the hips of some random girl I don't know.

I feel a pool of tears forming on my bottom lash line, but I press play anyway.

Andrew is still wearing the T-shirt that he had on when he came over for dinner tonight. I wonder if the girl grinding on him in the video could still smell the lasagna I made for him and Becca. Just when I thought it couldn't get worse, they start making out. Whoever was recording must have been trying to do it discreetly. You can see it by the way the camera is often blocked by a person passing by or someone's red solo cup from time to time. Their conversations are muffled, too; the only thing I can hear is the bass of a remixed song. But I don't need a clear shot or high-quality sound; I know what the fuck he's trying to show me. My boyfriend is shoving his tongue down another girl's throat while she's pressing her ass against his dick. A breathy gasp escapes my lips when I see Andrew walking away from the makeshift dance floor, only to open the door of, judging by the white tiles on the wall, the bathroom.

There must be an explanation for this. He must be drunk off his ass or maybe he tried drugs. His friends must be threatening him with a gun.

My heart sinks when he turns around to close the door and I see her palms on his stomach, tugging the shirt up as she feels up his abs. The damn thing almost stops working when I see him look in the direction of my secret good Samaritan and wink before closing the door.

CHAPTER 19

Luke

Last night was fucked up. What's even worse is Zoey almost walked in on us. Thank God for adjoining bathrooms. When we heard the knock on the other room, I basically ran to the bathroom and back into Kai's brother's bedroom.

I guess I'm not the only one who thinks it was a horrible idea. Gigi is avoiding me. If the fact that she skipped breakfast doesn't ring the alarm, the way she sent a text to the group chat saying she'll miss the tour of the farm Molly finished ten minutes ago certainly does.

"Where is Gigi?" I ask Zoey who's perched on the long, wooden dining table by the time I come back.

"Don't come near me," she says, her hair all tangled and her eyes glassy. "I think I have whatever Kai has."

"Need anything?"

Zoey shakes her head. "Just...can you check up on Gigi, please? She hasn't come down for breakfast and she's not answering her door." My body stiffens. *Did Gigi say anything to her last night?* "How much did you guys have to drink last night? She must be hungover as shit if she's still sleeping it off."

Exhaling a breath of relief, I give her a slight nod. "Get some rest, Zoey. I'll take care of her."

While my feet focus on going up, climbing the stairs two at a time, my mind is trying to figure out a way to tell Gigi in the nicest way possible that we can't have a repeat of what happened.

I mulled over the whole disaster last night when I couldn't sleep. This is wrong. In so many ways. She's my stepsister. And despite the fact that Andrew might have made a drunken mistake and hurt her, she should be with someone like him. Not the cheating part, but the popular and from a good family part. I wasn't made for Giuliana Bankowski; Andrew was.

Thinking about Andrew last night made me feel guilty like I've killed someone with my bare hands, but today...I'm just more confused than anything. Andrew had it all. To top it off, he had a beautiful and charming girlfriend. They were about to lose their virginities to each other? Why did he cheat on her? Did he kill himself because he felt bad for sleeping with Rachel? *Seems like a stupid way to die, especially if she forgave him. Why did she let him off the hook, anyway?*

Three knocks in and I hear a faint sound on the other end. "Come in."

I stand corrected. Gigi is not avoiding me.

"Hangover or stomach bug?" I ask when I see the bucket in the bathroom on the floor next to her bed.

"Stomach bug," she groans. "Definitely a stomach bug." Her voice is throaty, like she's been retching for hours.

I hesitate for a second before approaching her, but decide to do it, anyway. It's too late now, I'm probably going to be the fourth zombie in this house; my fate is already sealed. There's no point in keeping my distance anymore.

"You have a bit of a fever." Her forehead feels hot to the

touch. "I'll ask the others where the Tylenol is. What do you want to eat? There's soup and panini downstairs."

"You're a godsend," she says with her eyes closed, and I can't help the smile forming on my face.

"It's just soup and sandwich, Gi. Be right back."

When I enter her room for the second time, Gigi is crouching on the floor, her hands gripping the rim of the bucket. She looks at me and quickly wipes her mouth. "I'm disgusting."

"You're sick. Go clean yourself up, I'll empty this out."

"Luke," she drawls out my name. "You're not cleaning my puke. That's just gross."

"Gigi, just go change your shirt and brush your teeth. I've been cleaning up after Becca for as long as I can remember. You're good." I don't tell her that I did the same for Dad more times than I'd like to admit in the years he decided to try out being an alcoholic.

"You don't have to do this, you know," she says when I come back after rinsing the bucket in the downstairs bathroom. "Thank you, but it wasn't necessary."

"Do what?"

"Be nice to me. Take care of me now that I'm sick. I'm not your sister." *As if I didn't already know that.* "And if you're doing it because of last night..." She pauses, her gray eyes looking at the top of my cap, before daring to look at me straight. "I know what it was, Luke. I know how you operate."

I close the door behind me. I came here to tell Gigi that last night was a one-time thing, but I can't help but feel offended by what she's saying. *She knows how I operate?*

"What does that even mean?" My tone is harsh, probably too harsh for someone who's so sick she can't walk in a straight line back to her bed.

She tucks herself into bed before turning her face to me. "I went to *your* high school, Luke. I know what happens when girls sleep with you."

"And what is it that you think will happen, huh?" Crossing my arms over my chest, I feel the anger slowly building up inside of me. High school was a fucking horrible time in my life, but what did people in her grade even have to say about me? I kept my head down. No way people actually noticed me.

"You sleep with girls and then you ghost them."

If I were smart, I would use this moment to just go along with it. It's the perfect segue to my it-was-a-one-time-thing talk I've been preparing myself to have with Gigi. But my IQ seems to have depleted slightly ever since we walked into this ranch. So instead, I fuel my need to not seem like an asshole in front of the girl I just fucked last night and defend myself.

"That's not true," I scoff.

"So you telling Serena Taylor that you didn't have time for her, only one week after sleeping with her, is a lie?"

Serena Goddamn Taylor. A sophomore when I was a junior. I forgot she had to repeat a grade, that's probably how she and Gigi met. I still remember that day. I still remember the panic. The shame.

"That's true, but it's not the whole story," is all I manage to say.

"Well she wasn't the only one to tell me that you give zero fucks about the girls you bang."

I feel my lips tightening as I pinch the bridge of my nose. The deep breath that I'm taking seems to calm me down, not by a lot, though, but enough to continue this ridiculous conversation. The more I speak, the more I feel myself straying from my original goal of coming here. At this point, I don't give a shit anymore. I just don't want Gigi to think I'm an asshole. "It's not what you think." When she just raises her eyebrow but says nothing, I elaborate. "I had to take care of Becca. I didn't have the capacity to date."

"Capacity?" she asks, her tone unconvinced.

I scratch my head when I realize that it's a stupid word to describe the situation. "I had a lot of shit going on, alright? Does that explain it to you?" Feeling anger bubbling up at the memory, my tone becomes harsher than I want it to be. "You know what happened to my family."

And with that, I seem to manage to put an end to this conversation.

CHAPTER 20

Luke

SEVENTEEN YEARS OLD

SERENA

So are you going to come to the party or not?

I'm still thinking about it.

Come on, Luke. It's been a week since we've hung out. I only ever see you at school. Don't you want to have fun?

I'll try to make it, okay?

We'll pick you up. See you then!

Seeing my manager from the corner of my eye, I quickly shove my phone back inside the back pocket of my jeans and get back to the latte macchiato that I'm making.

"Order for Jamie is ready!" I yell.

By the time the person comes, I only give her a small smile, too busy trying to reduce the line in front of the counter.

Despite the chaos, I can't help but be chirpy. What can I say? I'm in a good mood. It's been a while since I've liked a girl. The last one was my first girlfriend—Amy Charmichaels. We dated for a few months before she lost interest in me. Although Andrew said it's all in my head, I'm pretty sure she hated that I spent more time with Becca than I did with her. Either that, or she finally connected the dots and figured out who I was and why we moved to Kinsdale Springs from Marble Crest all those years ago. The fire was a huge source of chatter in my old town and the surrounding areas, but Serena's family moved here a few years ago from out of state. That was one of the reasons why I liked her. When we got partnered up for chemistry, she looked at me like I was just a regular guy, not with pity in her eyes like some people or mockery like the bullies.

Humming to the tune of the song playing on the radio, I'm counting down the minutes until I'm out of here. One more hour and then it's clock out time. It's going to be tight, but if I hurry, I might be able to squeeze in a shower before Serena and her friends come to get me. With Becca's care sorted for the night, I might actually make it to my first high school party.

I shoot a quick text to Andrew, feeling like a complete idiot.

You've started partying, yeah?

ANDREW

That's a weird question.

How often do cops actually show up and bust these things? I can't afford to get arrested. I'm going to apply for scholarships next year. Need to be squeaky clean.

Stop watching dumb shit on TV and live it for yourself. Low chance.

As I'm wiping the counter, my phone vibrates in my pocket. It's longer this time. I frown when I see the caller ID.

"What's up, June?" I ask, clutching my phone using my cheek and my shoulder. "I can't really talk right now."

"It's...uh...it's your sister."

"Dad is supposed to pick her up today. I'm working."

"That's the thing, Luke. Vince isn't returning my calls and I have to go soon. Can you please get her?"

Sighing, I look at my manager who's already glaring at me. "I'll catch the next bus."

"Thank you." June hesitates, making sounds here and there on the other end, before finally letting her words out. "Happy birthday, Luke."

"You've got to be fucking kidding me," I mumble under my breath when I see Dad's sedan parked in front of the house.

"Another dollar for the curse jar!" Becca claps her hands, thinking she just won the lottery. God, she's so innocent. My sister is so damn happy all the time, oblivious to the mess that is our lives. My heart aches knowing that this charade won't last long—at least not if Dad keeps on going downhill.

The house is dark when we enter. I don't bother flicking the light switch on, knowing what I'm going to find slumped on the dining table. Pulling out my wallet, I take out some loose change and hand it to Becca. "Go count it upstairs and put it in the jar, alright? I'll be with you in a minute."

Becca nods happily, her eyes transfixed on the stupid coins. She's not even questioning why Dad's car is out front. Ignorance really is bliss. The moment I hear her door close upstairs, I make my way to the kitchen to face the music.

I turn on the hanging lamp that's directly on top of him. His body stirs as he groans. When he sees me leaning on the chair in front of him, he finally lifts his head up from the table, almost knocking the bottle of whisky off.

"You were supposed to pick Becca up, Dad." Not that he actually minds when he's not out of it. He loves my sister. It's me he has a problem with—the son who annihilated his family. At least he said as much a few weeks ago.

"Sorry, kid. I lost track of time." He slurs his words, so slowly and so painfully that I almost want to strangle him out of rage. When this is the stage he's in, it's not going to be long before he starts puking everywhere.

"Where the fuck were you?"

"I got fired." *Fuck my life.* "So I was busy looking for a new job," he says as he gestures toward the laptop on the table. Untouched and closed, still inside the sleeve.

"How did you get fired?" I already have an idea, but let's hear it from him. Let's see what fantasy he comes up with.

Dad has the audacity to unscrew the cap of his bottle and take another pull. "She said I was unfocused and tardy. The higher-ups never know what they're talking about." Never have I ever sympathized with middle management more than I do right now. *The amount of patience his manager must have had to let my dad continue his job as a bus driver instructor for this long...* How he has never gotten a DUI is a miracle.

"What's your plan?"

"I'll take a few weeks off. Maybe clean this place up a bit. Move around a few things."

I scoff at his stupid fucking idea. “You don’t have a few weeks, Dad. We’re barely making it as it is. In fact, we’re in minus with all the credit card debt.”

“What do you suggest I do, hm?” *Another sip.* “There is only one training facility in the area.”

“We can sell Grandma’s house.” My heart breaks hearing my own words. She left it to me. Grandparents aren’t supposed to have favorites, but she did. Lucas Palmer.

“Not until you finish college.” For all his horribleness, at least Dad loved his mom enough to remember her wish when she announced that I was going to inherit the place. Grandma was old-school and didn’t trust teenagers with a big sum of money. She made my parents and me swear up and down that I wouldn’t sell the house the first chance I got and blow through the money for a gap year or something stupid. “Besides, the bills aren’t paid *not* because we don’t have money. They’re not paid because I forgot. We still have some left from all the other houses we sold. You know, when your goddamn party killed everyone.” His chuckles pierce right through my chest. “I guess there’s an upside to everything. Isn’t that right, Luke?”

“Just give me the bills and your card details. I’ll handle it.” I don’t believe for a bit we haven’t plowed through our savings.

“Fine,” he grunts.

“What about the offer from Ross’s dad? He was asking whether you knew anybody who’d want to drive tour buses.”

“I took the instructor job for a reason, Luke,” he says, still slurring. “It’s so I don’t have to do long-haul trips anymore and be there for you two.”

My eyes are rolling so hard. I’m about to tell him to go fuck himself, but then the doorbell rings.

Serena Taylor is standing on my porch wearing the shortest dress I have ever seen someone wear.

Fuck, I forgot about her, I think to myself as I scrub my face, my grip still on the door handle.

Serena frowns when she sees me still in my Yellow Bird Coffee Shop T-shirt. "You're not ready?"

"I can't come, I'm sorry."

"But you said you would!"

"I said I'd try, but my sister is upstairs. I can't leave her alone." *Not with him like that.*

Serena quickly looks to the back, to her friends in the car, before giving me a cheeky smile. "What if I ditched them?" she asks in a whisper. "I can hang out with you guys."

I would love nothing more than to have her over and act like my house is not a stinking mess where my father is not three seconds away from dying of alcohol poisoning right there in the kitchen, but I don't want Serena to see me like this. What would she even think of me? When we hooked up, I saw how she lived. I saw the framed pictures on the wall. Serena Taylor would march right out if she saw the state my family is in.

"It's not a good idea." I'm at a loss with what I can tell this girl. *Sorry my life sucks? Sorry I can't do what other normal teenagers do? This will probably not go anywhere?*

"But it's your birthday," she whines.

I'm about to thank her for remembering, but the words are lodged in my throat the moment I hear a thud coming from inside the house. Panic takes over when footsteps come toward us.

"Who's your friend, Luke?"

Serena grins, probably thinking she's about to meet the parents. Fuck, if I don't do something, she probably will. "Serena, you have to go. I'll see you at school."

"But I j—"

"I don't have time for this, Serena."

"Who is it?" Dad asks again.

Before he can walk past me, I make a split-second decision and shout, "Just some friend. She's leaving."

Kinsdale Springs and the bordering areas are a tight-knit community. A lot of the locals already know why we moved here. They don't need to know that, on top of the doom and gloom surrounding our family, Vincent Palmer turned into a disgusting slob of an alcoholic.

CHAPTER 21
Gigi

"UH, WHAT THE FUCK, GUYS?" I HEAR A MASCULINE voice somewhere.

"Holy crap." I think that's Zoey's voice because the giggles that follow are familiar. I've heard it a million times before.

I slowly open my eyes, but it doesn't take long before they widen, doubling in size. Luke is next to me, still softly snoring. His arm is draped along the width of my waist and our legs are tangled together. His skin is burning and there are beads of sweat running down the side of his face. It takes a second for me to register what happened last night. *Luke told me a story about Serena, Luke starting to puke, me telling Luke to just stay here with me.*

"Earth to Gigi!" My best friend's voice rings loud in my right ear again.

I look over Luke's head next to mine and sure enough, both of our friends are standing in the middle of the room. Kai has a shit-eating grin on his face and Zoey is giving me a *what the hell happened in here* look.

Luke's leg jerks just as I am propping myself up on my

elbows. Zoey's mouth gapes when Luke tightens his hold on me. "Let's sleep a little longer, Gi."

Laughing nervously, I poke his arm with my index finger. "Luke." No answer, so I call out his name again, louder this time. "Luke."

"What?" he asks in a raspy voice, his eyes still closed.

"We've got company."

A moment later, he must register what I'm trying to say, because his honey eyes open, panic filing them. He stiffens before turning his head to the bedroom door.

"Wakey, wakey, Lukey," Kai teases.

"Well, shit." Luke scrubs his face with his palm.

The four of us just stare at each other in silence, not knowing what to say. That is until Malakai breaks out in laughter so loud it echoes through the halls of the house. "So this is a thing, huh?"

In typical Luke fashion, he doesn't say anything to that, keeping his poker face on. *Is he waiting for me to say something?*

"It's not a big deal." I shrug, offering Luke an out. I instigated, I should be the one taking care of the mess. "People do it all the time. You two do it all the time."

"Not with my brother I don't," Zoey chimes in, barely keeping a straight face as she bites her lips to keep her from laughing. "So, just so we're clear on what's *not* a big deal. You two banged, right?

Luke groans next to me. "She's not my sister." He doesn't dignify her question with an answer, but they know. I know they know.

"And that's not the problem, either," I blurt out before stopping myself. When the three of them turn to me for an explanation, I swallow it down and save myself by saying, "We were drunk. Now pick your jaws up from the floor and let's go down and have breakfast. That's why you two are here, no?"

The problem is the person no one talks about anymore. Luke reminds me of him just like I remind Luke of him. *Is that why I wanted to sleep with Luke? Is that why he fucked me?* My head hurts spinning in circles. I had sex with a Palmer. *Just not the one that I was supposed to.*

CHAPTER 22
Luke

Two weeks have gone by since the God-awful trip. Two weeks since I have tried my best to avoid Gigi. Or Gigi, me. I think she's putting in more effort to skip parties and mutual hangs than I am. Nobody needs to write that many papers. Not even Miss Busy Bee Bankowski.

Kai and Zoey mocking us the rest of the stay was probably enough for her to steer clear of me. If their reaction is any indication of how the whole world will react to us sleeping together, *yeah...fuck that*. I'll take it to my grave. Except I can't get her out of my head.

I used to look at Gigi in another light, I swear. How did this happen? We had a one-night stand and suddenly, she's all I think about.

It's probably just the guilt, Luke, I say to myself while I towel dry my hair. Grabbing my duffel bag out of the locker, I pass through the equipment and students finishing up their workout sessions before the place closes down at midnight.

I still can't believe that sometimes this is my life. My scholarship allows me to have so much free time sometimes I don't even know what to do with my day. The small stipend they transfer to my bank account each month frees me from having to search for a part-time job. Going to the gym, going to parties, and getting eight hours' worth of sleep are things that I was never able to do back home. Gigi was right, I am a late bloomer.

Banging the car door shut, I curse to myself when I catch where my mind is off to. *You're fucking thinking about Gigi. Again.*

The drive to my off-campus apartment that I share with Malakai does nothing to calm the conflicting thoughts. Especially not when I see none other than the person of interest herself in a white button-down shirt that hides her perfect, tiny tits and a black pencil skirt paired with see-through tights that do nothing to cover the curve of her ass. Gigi is clutching her jacket with her thighs as she puts her headphones over her head. Before I can think twice, I pull over next to her and roll down my windows.

"What are you doing here?"

It's a stupid question. We both know that I know she works at the restaurant she's standing in front of. After recovering from her startle, she humors me and answers anyway. "Got the dinner shift."

"You heading home, Gi?"

She nods. You can feel the air thickening around us in the silence that comes after. Our eyes lock, trying to speak the words we can't. I don't know how she feels about me, and I wish she would just fucking tell me. I wish we were closer so I could read her facial expression. Very hypocritical of me considering the fact I've done nothing to start the conversation. I didn't even do as much as send her a text after that trip. The only interaction we've had is through the group chat that we all share within our merged friend group and that one time we saw each other at the library. Christ, I've done nothing but prove the rumors about me right.

"Get in. I'll take you home."

"Oh, it's fine," she says with a nervous laugh. "I don't mind walking."

"It's eleven at night. Please, just get in. It's a fucking car ride, not a marriage proposal."

She cocks an eyebrow, and I cock one right back at her. Opening the door from the inside, I make my intention clear that I'm not going to drive away until she's inside. Gigi throws her purse on the seat before looping her headphones around her neck and jumping in, closing the door next to her.

Even with all the awkwardness, you can always count on Giuliana Bankowski to always put in an effort to break the ice. "So, how have you been?" she asks. When she sees the corner of my lip quirk upward as I steal a glance to look at her, she smiles back. "What? I can't ask how you're doing?"

"Are you just asking for the sake of it or do you really want to know?"

"You're making this weird, Luke."

"What?" I ask in a playful tone not matching my stammering heartbeat caused by having this girl in my car. Right now, it doesn't feel like we're in a tangled web of chaos, it just feels like we're two college kids who had sex over spring break and we're doing the post-hookup, awkward dance. "Since you've been doing everything in your power to avoid me, it's a fair question don't you think?"

"What?" She pretends to be offended, pointing a finger to her chest. "If anybody is avoiding anyone, it's you. You didn't even come to Zach's birthday party two days ago."

I will myself to hold my tongue. I take a deep breath to calm myself down. I try talking myself out of it. I lost. "I can't stop thinking about what happened, Gi."

I can't see her because I'm focused on the road, but I think she's gawking at me. "In a good way or a bad way?" she asks in a soft voice, like she's afraid of what my answer will be.

"Is it bad if I think about what we did in a good way?" I ask, surprising even myself.

"Is it because I was a virgin?" Gigi blurts out, sounding more confident than she was five seconds ago. "Like a fetish thing?"

I can't help the snort that comes through my nose and mouth, accompanied by my silent chuckles. "Maybe. I don't know."

"Well I'm not one anymore, thanks to you. Sorry, Luke, you can't devirginize me twice."

"Have you...did you sleep with anyone else after—"

"No," she cuts me right off.

"Huh."

"What?"

"Nothing," I answer, pulling the car to a stop once we reach her building. "A part of me thought you slept with me just so that you can finally get it over with. I thought for sure you hooked up with Pierre at Zach's party. You guys looked all cozy in the pictures."

"Is Lucas Palmer jealous?" When I turn to face her, rolling my eyes, I see the taunting written all over her face. *She's enjoying this.* "I didn't know you were the jealous type. From all the stories I've heard, you seemed like the hit it and quit it type of guy."

"Fuck the stories," I groan. "I thought I cleared the air when I told you about Serena. If you want to know something, ask it from the source."

"Okay. Have you slept with anyone else since we did it?"

I shake my head. It seems like what I confessed to her didn't get through her skull, so I reiterate. "Like I said, I couldn't stop thinking about you." Still can't.

"On a scale of one to ten, how hard was it for you to admit that to me, Luke?" Gigi asks with a satisfied grin.

"Hard enough." Fair is fair. "But it's true. And for the

record, it's not just because you were a virgin. You're pretty cool, Gi. Sorry I never gave you a chance before."

"Now that must have been excruciatingly painful for you to say."

"You're a pain in the ass, you know that?" I laugh.

After a beat of silence, Gigi says what we're all fucking thinking. "You know this is wrong, right?"

"I know."

"For the record, I also can't stop thinking about what happened." I feel the sudden rush of relief washing over me. Relief that's laced with uncertainty and guilt. The kind that keeps you up at night. Gigi plants a kiss on my cheek before climbing out of my car. "Thanks for the ride, Luke. I'll try not to avoid you next time."

"Hey, Gi!" I shout from inside the truck. "What are you doing this weekend? And don't say you have to do some bullshit paper."

"Absolutely nothing." We both smile at her answer.

"Go with me somewhere?"

"Like a...date?"

"Yeah," I answer, already knowing what I have to do. "Something like that."

CHAPTER 23
Gigi

I BITE MY BOTTOM LIP AS I LOOK AT MYSELF IN THE mirror. This is my third outfit change. He's going to be here any minute now.

When Luke and I had the talk a few days ago, I didn't expect the night to end with him asking me out on a date. Luke was right; aside from Zach's birthday party that I couldn't miss, I had been avoiding places and events that I knew he would be at. Although Luke confessed to me that he didn't really take things further with girls he messed around with in high school because he just didn't have the capacity, their stories match the image of Luke I had in my head for so long—the aloof and douchey one. What we did was already confusing. I didn't want to hurt my feelings and make the situation murkier, so I took the easy way out.

I should have known. Asshole or no asshole, nothing comes easy when it comes to Lucas Palmer.

LUKE

I'm outside.

Brushing my hair to the side, I sigh. *Think of happy thoughts, Gigi. Picture the ocean. Picture the park...*I can't bring myself to finish my words of affirmation, because, well, how can I? How can I when tonight feels like the ultimate betrayal to Andrew? Luke was his best friend. For heaven's sake, Luke was his *cousin*. I argue with myself for a few seconds that *second* cousin is not really that bad, but then I remember who Luke is. My stepbrother. *I am so fucked.*

I study psychology, but what I really need is a therapist. Not a way to become one. Me chucking a few condoms in my bag right now just for good measure really drives the point home.

After excusing everything in my head—using the fact that Luke and I have never actually lived under one roof, aren't blood-related, and before college, have only met a handful of times—I shake away all the legitimate reasons that I should cancel and stride my way down the hall.

Luke's truck is sitting in the parking lot with the interior light turned on, giving me a glimpse of him on his phone. "Hey," he says when I open the passenger door. "You're here."

"You asked me out?"

He backs out of the parking space. Once we're on the road, Luke finally speaks, his gaze focused on the road. "For a second there, I thought you were going to bail on me."

For a second there, I thought the same. "Are you disappointed I showed up?"

He shoots me a lazy smile that turns my stomach into knots. "Nah," he says, shaking his head. "I'm glad you did."

"Where are we going?"

"You'll see," is all he says. The glint in his eyes is making my fingers tingle. This is just one date. I'm getting ahead of myself, but would we even work in real life without the complications? I'm a people person and Luke, well, he's Luke.

College seems to be loosening him up a bit, but he's still the same guy on the inside. Stoic and perpetually nonchalant.

The rest of the drive goes exactly like I imagined it would —with Luke not giving me any details as to where we're heading and me probing every chance I get. Half an hour goes by when Luke finally parallel parks on a street in a town I haven't been to.

"You can stop with the questions now, Gi," he says, pulling the brakes. "We're here."

I almost squeal our ears off when I see the neon sign on my right. Grandma's Cat Café. "How did you know?" I turn my head to him, my hand already about to pry open the car door.

Luke just shrugs. "It's not hard to figure you out. Do you know how often you post on your socials about wanting a cat?" I blush at the thought of Luke seeing my rants online. *He checks out my profile.* "Well what are we waiting for? We didn't drive all the way here just to sit in the car, did we?" he asks, bringing me out of my own head.

After ordering, I immediately play with Mr. Whiskers and Teddy, the two black cats that are circling our small table in the corner.

"He's so cute." I make kissy faces while cuddling Teddy, cradling him like a baby.

Luke pets Mr. Whiskers, who jumped on his lap, his big hand stroking the fur on the cat's back. "Your mom never allowed you to have a pet, huh?"

"Nope. She's allergic. Besides, we weren't allowed to have pets in our building back in New York." This is why I love small towns more. People have their own places, more freedom. I hadn't even seen big backyards until I moved to Kinsdale Springs. My friends in New York who live in houses all live in dense areas. "What about you? Why did you guys never have a pet?"

"Too much work. Becca wanted to get a dog, but realistically, who would have taken care of the dog?"

I was about to say *you could help her* when I realize how wrong that would be. I let go of Teddy to tap my nails on the table when the gears in my brain start turning. It's stupid, but it never occurred to me how much Luke must have done for his family growing up. When he said he didn't have the capacity to be in relationships during high school, I thought it was because he was too busy studying, or it was because of his grief. But his mom is gone, and his dad is a long-distance tour bus driver. He must have been the primary caretaker of Becca before we moved. Of course he didn't have time to go to prom and date around.

"Why do you never visit Becca?" I ask, changing the atmosphere composition from light to heavy. *Gigi, you should have just kept your mouth shut.*

To my surprise, Luke cocks an eyebrow as he sips on his lemonade through the straw. His expression is cool as a cucumber as he continues petting Mr. Whiskers, like my question doesn't bother him. "Who says I don't?"

"I would know? I lived with her for almost two years?"

"But you don't go to church with her," he says in an amused tone. He's not wrong. Andrew's mom always picks Becca up every Sunday to go with her in their town. On the odd occasion that I did go to church, I go to the Catholic one with Mom. Otherwise, I'm more of an Easter and Christmas kind of believer.

"So what? You drive there every Sunday? I find it hard to believe that you're that religious."

"I'm not," he answers. "I just go there to see my sister. Once a month when I can." When he continues, the tone of his voice changes. "And Andrew's parents."

Guilt bubbles up inside me, but not in the way I have been anticipating. Andrew used to skip church when we were together, and it annoyed the hell out of his parents. In the beginning, it was because we wanted to spend all our free time together, which was hard to do with my cheer practice and his basketball training unless it was on the weekends. Then, he just didn't go for the sake of not going. In hindsight, those were his last moments I stole away from his family. *From Luke.*

CHAPTER 24
Luke

She's acting weird. Maybe it's all in my head, but I thought the first half of our date went pretty great, but at some point Gigi just lost interest, only speaking when I asked her questions and using the cats as an excuse to ignore me. And now we're here, back in the car, and I know for a fact the reason she's turning the volume up is not because she wants to listen to whatever crap is playing on the radio.

"Did I do something to piss you off?" I ask once we reach a red light.

Playing with the flap of her sling bag, she looks at ongoing traffic for a second before looking at me, her gray eyes almost silver from the taillight shining in front of us. "So I stole Andrew from you, huh?" she finally says.

Oh. *Oh*. "We both know that's not true."

"But it is, right? That's why you're always pissed at me."

"What are you talking about?" I scoff, stealing one last glance at her before driving straight ahead. "I am not pissed at you."

"But you were," she argues.

"Yes, I was. But I'm not anymore."

"What changed? Except for the fucking." *God, this girl is so bold.*

"I think I was just mad at the world, Gi."

"Why?"

Because I feel guilty for what happened to my family. Because I was the reason my father lost his wife. Because I sometimes got jealous of Andrew for being the golden Palmer son. "Maybe another day, okay?" I say in a soft tone when I catch her pouting. Without realizing what I'm doing, I pull her hand, intertwining her delicate fingers with mine.

"What are you doing, Luke?" she asks, unsure.

"Did you have fun tonight?" I ask, ignoring her question.

"I did. The cats were really cute. You did good." Gigi smiles, and I gradually feel the tension in the car disappear. "Thank you."

"Do you want to hang at my place?" When she cocks her eyebrow, I chuckle a bit. "I think Kai is in your dorm right now. We can watch a movie and wait them out. I'll drive you back."

Three hours in and Kai still hasn't replied to any of my texts, asking when they'd finish fucking. Gigi locks her phone and throws it on the bed. "Zoey said it's going to take a while. They're not doing the dirty, by the way. They're fighting."

I guess that's our cue to continue with *The Ring*. "I just need to take a piss. You can watch without me."

When I come back, Gigi is lying on her side wrapped in my blanket. Her eyes keep fluttering as she fights to stay awake, only half paying attention to the movie playing on the mounted TV in front of the bed. I take my previous spot next to her beside the wall. My hand itches to play with the strands of her inky, black hair, to feel the sleek texture with the pad of my thumb.

"People in horror movies are so dumb," she says, breaking me out of my daze.

"You think so?"

"Yep. Why on Earth would you walk into a dark room or follow the sound of a voice, knowing full well that there is a ghost haunting you?" Gigi turns around to face me, and like the hopeless loser that I am, I slump down so that our heads are at the same level. "I'd probably do the same, though. I'd probably just surrender if a ghost were to haunt me. Dying is better than having that creepy girl chase me around."

We're so close now that I feel her pinky on the side of my thigh. Inside, I'm panicking like some high school kid who has a girl over for the first time. This awfully feels like a date a fifteen-year-old would have.

"Luke?"

"What?"

"What are you doing?"

I look down and finally see what she's staring at: my arm around her stomach. I don't remember doing that. *When did that happen?* Instead of pulling it away, I pull her closer to me so that we're spooning. Her ass wriggles around and I close my eyes, hoping she doesn't feel the boner that's growing in my jeans.

We watch the movie in silence until Gigi finally speaks. "Luke." My name comes out in a sigh.

"Yeah?"

"What are we doing?" She doesn't sound like she's about to ask me to take her home. She doesn't sound angry. She sounds confused, and honestly, I can relate. *Big time.*

"I don't know." No manual. No guidebook. "All I know is I really want to kiss you right now."

"Then do it," she whispers.

I caress her cheek with my thumb as I stare into her sleepy eyes. The fact that Naomi Watts is being chased by a girl that comes out of a TV doesn't distract me from appreciating the fact that Gigi is looking at me like she'd rather be here than anywhere else right now. She's so fucking gorgeous.

When I catch her lower lip with my mouth, she closes her eyes and kisses me back. Her hands roam over my shirt, taking in my back, before moving to my arm and then down to my abs. She whimpers as one of mine goes under her sweater, grazing her nipple under her bra.

I overheard her telling Zoey once that she's insecure about her tiny breasts. "I love your tits," I say, pulling my lips away from her, before unhooking the strap on her back. Lowering my head down, I suckle on her hardened peaks, my tongue circling the brown part of the skin.

Gigi squirms around as she runs her hand through my locks. "I love that you grew out your hair."

"Yeah?" I ask with a smile as I unbutton her jeans. "I'll keep that in mind." *Is she asking because Andrew used to keep his hair like this?*

Trailing kisses down her stomach, I'm about to take her panties off when she stops me in my tracks. "Just fuck me, Luke. Please."

"Why don't you want to get licked out?" I ask, almost not believing this. There's a first time for everything, but not this. There should never be a first time for this.

The skin of her pale face turns a shade of pink. "I...I'm embarrassed." Who would have known? The great Giuliana Bankowski is human, after all.

"Of how you taste?"

"No, no." She shakes her head. "I, uh, I can't come...when someone fingers me. Also when, uh...I get eaten out. You're putting in effort for nothing, so spare yourself the work."

I stop my laughter when I realize she's dead serious. *What the actual fuck?* "Will you let me try?" I ask with a smile. She nods, but when I start peppering kisses on her shaved part, she leans on her elbow as if she's getting ready to tell me to stop wasting my time again. "Just relax, Gi. Lie back down and try to enjoy, okay?"

I slide a finger inside her pink opening, feeling her wetness covering my skin. Drawing lazy circles on her clit, I kiss each of her parted knees. "Close your eyes," I tell her gently. "I'll take care of you, I promise." Something that I should have done when I fucked her for the first time.

I lean on my free arm as my finger works on her and my eyes watch how she reacts. Gigi obeys me. Her eyes are closed, but by the way her eyebrows are scrunched together, I can tell she's holding back. With my finger still on her, I lie on my side next to her and caress her hair. "You've never had an orgasm in your life, have you?" The puzzle pieces finally click in place.

"Is it really that obvious?" she asks, finally letting her guard down.

"Even with Andrew?"

"No," she finally breathes the truth into the room.

"I'm going to eat you out and you're going to relax. Don't think too much with that brain of yours. Just ride it out, can you do that?"

"Okay, yeah." She flashes me a small smile. "I can try."

My tongue moves in slow, deliberate motions. I am completely sober this time around and I have all night to make her come. She's not walking out of this room without an orgasm. After a few minutes, she's scooting up. It seems like her brain is finally catching up to her. I gently pull her hips back to me, locking them in as I take more wetness from inside of her and drag it up to her clit. Gigi moans when I do that. She does it again when I start sucking on her swollen bud. When her back arches and she's about to lean on her elbow again, I replace my mouth with my finger to do the work.

"Don't fight it."

She closes her eyes again and I decide to try something different. With two of my fingers still playing with her clit, I hover over her and catch one of her nipples in my mouth. She loved it before, maybe this will do it for her. My dick is painfully strained behind the zipper of my jeans when Gigi starts whimpering. *I'm about to give Gigi her first orgasm.* I keep going when she starts cursing. I don't stop when she starts trembling beneath me. I smile when her body finally goes limp.

"Now that wasn't so bad, was it?" I smile before giving her a short kiss on the lips.

"No." She laughs. "No, it wasn't."

Fucking her after that is also a different affair than it was the first time around. Unlike last time, I take my time with her. Sliding in and out of her slowly in missionary as I take a good look at the girl trapped under my body. Gigi holds my face with both of her hands, not shying away from me watching her. When I feel the warm sensation slowly spreading from my lower back, I pick up the pace. Gigi hooks her legs around my waist as I push into her, taking each thrust with our lips locked together.

"Fuck, Gi. Fuck," I say through heavy breaths when my climax comes, burying my head in the crook of her neck. "You're on the shot, right?" I ask, realizing that we didn't use a condom. *Again.*

Relief washes over me when she whispers a yes before kissing my cheek, her lips covered in beads of sweat.

My dick is still semi-hard when I roll over, giving her enough room to be the little spoon again. I'm about to remind her to go pee when she takes my hand in hers, pulls me close, and calls out my name softly. "Luke."

"Hm?"

"If we're going to do this again, I need you to do something for me." *Have sex without a condom? Have sex in general? Where is she going with this?*

"Name your price." I'll happily sell my kidney on the black market at this point.

"I need you to open up to me. I can't do this if you don't let me in." Gigi pauses for a second before continuing. "Be intimate, I mean."

Kissing the crown of her head, I hold her tighter. "I'll let you in."

CHAPTER 25

Gigi

THEY SHOULDN'T BE CALLING THIS A PAJAMA PARTY. I'd bet all the money in the world that these are not the outfits these students wear to bed. I know I'm not wearing my usual sweatpants and tank top. They shouldn't label tonight as a fundraiser, either. Although it might be true that all the money in the donation box by the front door will be given to charity, nobody in this house cares about the underprivileged. Everybody just wants to get hammered.

"Here." Zach hands me a drink. "Vodka tonic."

"Thanks," I answer curtly, still feeling somewhat salty that he managed to guilt-trip me into coming here. The only thing I wanted to do after coming home from work was curl up in bed, but he sent me an SOS text. It turns out Zach and I have different definitions of the term. I thought he was in one of his depressive episodes again, the ones that seem to come out of nowhere and make him sulk for a few days at a time. He thought a girl ghosting him after five days was enough to warrant sending me the message. After what happened with Andrew, the alarm bells in my head always ring every time someone tells me they're depressed, even if they're just exaggerating.

Maybe I'm a magnet for these types of people, but my best guy friend seems to be the one to always ring said bell.

"So what happened with the girl from your ancient civilizations course again?" I ask, tipping the cup to my lips.

"I don't know. One moment we're talking about going on a double date with Zoey and Kai, and the next thing I know, she won't return my calls."

"Maybe you read the vibes wrong."

"Me?" He gives me a smug grin. "Never." I love him to death, but why do these guys who play football seem to be overconfident all the time? It's like the coach mixes their protein powder with arrogance or something. The moment someone tells them no or something doesn't go their way, they either get shitfaced like Zach right now or throw a temper tantrum. "Anyway, why are you not interested in Pierre again?" *There it is. Point proven.*

"Zach." I close my eyes so I can curb my urge to say something mean. "He's looking for a fling and I'm...not looking. Period. You have to stop setting us up. You're making the both of us uncomfortable at this point."

"What happened to *hey, I'm Gigi and I'm ready to get back out there*?"

"I am," I answer, feeling the panic slowly taking over my body. *I did tell him that at the beginning of the year before... Luke happened.* "Just not with Pierre. He'll be leaving the US in the summer."

Do I stop dating now that Luke and I are doing things? Are we dating? We've fucked twice and text on the regular now. We even met once on Tuesday in a group setting. But ever since he gave me my first-ever orgasm last week, we haven't really talked much about what we actually are. We mostly just talk about unimportant things like how our classes are and what dinner we're eating that day. He also hasn't asked me out again.

"I didn't know he was back with Autumn," Zach asks suddenly.

"Who?" I ask, still preoccupied with my own thoughts.

"Luke." *Well, he has my attention now.*

I think I might be hearing him wrong, but sure enough, when I follow his gaze to the lawn of the sorority house, I spot them. Luke, Autumn, Zoey, and Malakai all taking a shot from a tray being held by some freshman I know from one of my classes. Luke and Kai are wearing flannel pajama pants in different colors while Zoey is wearing a nightgown and Autumn is covered in the same pattern that Luke has on his bottoms. My heart sinks. *Did they decide to wear a matching set?*

"I didn't know either," I mumble. "Zach, I think I'm going to head—"

"Yo, guys!" Zach yells in their direction. *Fuck*. "We're here!"

Out of the three of them, Luke is the only one who's not smiling when he sees us. He shoves one hand in his pocket and follows the other three in our direction.

"Gigi!" Zoey squeals. "I thought you said you weren't coming."

"Yeah, Zach made me come," I say, trying my best not to glare at Luke and Autumn. Just because I'm not looking at him, doesn't mean that I don't feel him burning a hole on the side of my head. He might as well be shooting laser beams with those eyes of his.

"Giuliana Bankowski here," Zach slurs. "Is just trying to be a good wingwoman for me tonight. Layla ghosted me."

"So no double date then?" Kai asks, crinkling his nose.

"Give me a few weeks." Zach smirks. "I'm sure I can come

up with something." And I have no doubt he will. This guy is one good-looking, giant bear.

"And when you do," Autumn chimes in. "Maybe we can triple date." I tip back my cup and drink the rest of my vodka tonic. As I'm swallowing, what she says makes me want to throw everything back up. "Right, Luke?"

Luke doesn't answer. Since everyone's focus is on him, waiting for his response, I summon the courage to look at him as well. *Safety in numbers, right?* I suck in a breath when I see his hardened stare pinned on me, like he's daring me to say something. I almost scoff at him. What does he think I'm going to do? Stake my claim? *Or maybe he's silently pleading with me to keep my mouth shut.*

"Gonna get myself a refill," I announce with a fake smile, lifting my cup in the air. When I pass by the freshman handing out the shots, I grab one and take it. It's not enough to make me forget what Luke and I did or what Autumn just said, but it's enough to keep me warm for my walk home in this late April weather.

CHAPTER 26
Luke

"She's in a mood," Autumn says, none the wiser, watching Gigi gulp down the disgusting pink liquid from the shot glass she just took.

Kai and Zoey both shift uncomfortably in their positions. Zoey has her phone out. She's texting Gigi, no doubt. When Gigi gets on her tiptoes to unhook her jacket from the hanger by the front door, Zoey moves her feet.

"I'll go," I say immediately, raising my hand in front of her chest.

Zoey looks like she's about to say something, but it's Autumn who speaks instead. "Just let Zoey go after her. They're heading in the same direction, anyway."

"Two girls walking at this time of night might not be a fucking good idea, actually," Kai tries to interfere.

"We're on campus. What's the worst that can happen?" Autumn shrugs. *Don't throttle her, Luke.*

Gigi is on the front porch now, and once she turns left, she'll be out of our sight. I need to go after her. Before walking to grab my own jacket, I finally give my ex-girlfriend a piece of my mind. "Autumn, just drop it, okay? I've told you a fucking thousand times already. No. Fucking go out with Zach or something, then you all can have your double date." Autumn's mouth hangs open. Softening my tone, I speak again. "Sorry, but I can't."

I might have just clued in Autumn and Zach on our secret. They're not idiots; they're going to figure this one out sooner or later. I don't care. What I care about is getting to Gigi before she overthinks this and decides that I am exactly like the rumors people at Kinsdale Springs High fed her.

"Gigi," I call out when I see her about to cross the road. She doesn't turn back, choosing to take bigger steps instead. "Gigi, wait." Nope. Not slowing down. She walks faster, even. "Gi, just fucking stop!"

When I finally catch up to her, I hold her wrist. She turns, showing me her red-rimmed eyes. "Let go of me," she whispers.

"Gigi, please," I say, still trying to catch my breath. Jogging in the middle of the night after a pizza dinner and a few shots wasn't in the cards tonight. "It's not what you think it is."

Tears fall down her face, but she quickly rubs them away with the palm of her hand. "It's not the first time I've heard that sentence from a Palmer," she scoffs. *Truly, just fuck.*

"I didn't cheat on you." I try to pull her closer, but she shoves me away.

"You just cheated on *Autumn* with me."

"No." Exhaling a sigh, I make sure that my tone is not raised. "There is nothing going on with me and Autumn. I promise."

Gigi snorts, still marching in the direction of her dorm, and I'm still going after her like a guilty man begging for forgiveness. "Then what was that about, huh? You two look awfully cozy for people who broke up when you were sophomores." I hate that the only time I went back home during that year I brought Autumn along with me. She must have heard it from her mom. I never bring girls back. I can't imagine what's going through Gigi's mind right now.

"Look, I slept with her last year after the funeral," I admit. "And I think I gave her the wrong impression. But I haven't done anything with her since, I promise."

She slows her pace down, but her jaw is still tight. "Don't let me stop you. We're not together."

"Is that how you're going to play it, really?"

She doesn't answer. I call out her name, but she ignores me as she looks for her keys inside her jacket pocket. When she unlocks the front door to her building, I follow her in.

"How else should I play it, Luke?" she hisses in a whisper. "We're not together. We can't be together. You're my step-brother, for God's sake."

In the school compound, two hours away from Kinsdale Springs, it's easy to forget our reality. To forget the ties that bind me and her. I hate that she's bringing it up because I'm past the point of caring.

"If I wasn't?"

"Well you are," she quips.

I'm not used to this—expressing myself, pleading, whatever. There is a small voice in my head telling me, though, if I don't use my words, I might never turn this situation around.

"I don't care."

"If you weren't, you'd still be Andrew's cousin."

"Don't care about that, either." He left us. Andrew left us without a goodbye. If he cared about any of us, he wouldn't have fucking done that. I'm not about to make her even sadder by saying that, so instead I say, "He would want us to be happy."

"It's wrong," she answers with a tired voice, looking relieved that she's finally in her own room.

"Gigi, look," I plead, using the last argument in my back pocket. "You wanted me to let you in. I'm letting you in. I haven't been able to stop thinking about you since the farm. I can't stop. I just can't. I'm happy when I'm with you. Please, just give me a chance."

"What about Autumn?" *She can't be fucking serious. This is what she's going with now?*

"Don't care about her, too. I don't want to be with anyone else but you."

"I'm scared, Luke," she says in a voice barely above a whisper. "You and I both know this is not going to end well."

"You'll never know if you don't give this a shot."

She eyes me skeptically. Her head is tilted to the side as if she can't believe the words that are coming from my mouth. "And what would that look like?" she asks with one hand on her hip. "Us giving this a shot? Because I don't want to be your dirty little secret. I don't want to see girls like Autumn all over you at parties while I'm stuck pretending that I'm single and not totally falling for you."

She wants me, too. "You're falling for me?" I can't help the smile on my face.

"Well, uh," she mumbles, trying to find the words that will get her out of this. "Saying I'm crushing on you sounds like I'm twelve."

"Weak argument," I say, grinning.

Gigi rolls her eyes. "Whatever. You're an asshole."

Pulling the waistband of her satin pajama pants, I bring her closer to me. I tuck a loose strand of her hair behind her ear before bringing our foreheads together. "Nobody says we have to sneak around. We're surrounded by thirty-five thousand other students, Gi. Nobody gives a shit about us."

"I don't want to hide you, Luke."

I bring my lips to hers, tasting the bubblegum-flavored shot she drank back at the party. Gigi has a way of sucking people into her orbit, using her charm, and making them feel loved. I don't think she notices the power she has over her family and friends. I've seen it with my own eyes. She's done it to Andrew, to Zoey, to Becca, to Zach…and she's doing it to me. I'm not going to fight how I feel. Maybe we really did fuck the first time for the wrong reasons. It doesn't change anything now. I want this. I want her.

"Let's not hide, then."

CHAPTER 27

Gigi

It doesn't happen that often that Zoey and I eat lunch alone. When we're not tagging along with Kai, Luke, and their other friends who are juniors, we always eat with Zach. But Luke has a presentation today and Zach is looking for Layla's replacement, which is why he's sitting way at the back, trying his best to impress his date with his muscles. I'm not complaining; I think the two of us could really use some girl time, especially now.

"So what's going on with you and Kai?" I ask my sulking roommate who's just pushing her chicken pieces around.

"I think we're going to break up." Zoey puts her fisted hand under her chin and sighs. "Ever since we went to his place during spring break, all he can talk about is how great that place is and how he can't wait to move back home once he's done with college."

I can't really blame him. His family's farm is amazing. I spent most of the time that week confined to the bedroom with puke all over my hair, but still...I understand where he's coming from. "Doesn't really match your plan of wanting to move to Seattle, does it?"

"It's stupid," she says in a tone that makes my heart break for her. "I don't even know why we keep on fighting about this. He keeps on telling me to move with him after I finish school, but I'm nineteen, Gigi! I still have three more years here. Besides, I don't want to live in the boonies."

"Sorry to say this, Zo." I pause, grimacing, not sure whether I should continue or not. "He's probably bringing all of this up because next year is going to be his last year here. I'd be worried if he's not thinking about his future right now." *Tough love, it is.*

Zoey rolls her eyes as she groans. "I hate it when you're right."

"Maybe you can tell him to shelve the topic first. I don't know, for a later date or something? And see where it goes with the two of you until then."

We eat in silence since she's not in a talkative mood. Zoey keeps on checking her phone, probably waiting for a text from Kai. I've never seen her like this—sad. She's usually perky and the life of the party, even more so than me.

I'm finishing my pudding when my own phone vibrates in my pocket.

LUKE

Presentation went great. Where are you?

I knew you could do it! Lunch. Don't come, though. Zoey is in a mood.

Kai?

Yep. She'll shoot you just by association.

She can try. I'm hungry and I miss you.

Clutching my phone with my two hands, I feel a smile

forming on my lips. I miss him, too. He's been so busy preparing for today and I have been cramped with an assignment from my cognitive development course; I feel like it's been ages since we've been together. With Zoey and Kai on the rocks, the group doesn't meet that often anymore.

What did you say about Becca again? I thought it's impossible to miss someone when you talk to them almost every day? ;)

LUKE

I stand corrected. What are you doing tonight?

Dinner shift :(Pick me up? You can tell me all about today.

You work too much.

Not everyone can be as smart as you, Luke. Not all of us get a monthly allowance from the Daedalus Foundation.

Alright. I don't want you to walk alone at night, anyway.

I don't know what it is about Luke. He doesn't shower me with compliments, nor does he give me cute pet names. His love language is not words of affirmation. But when he does say something, like *you work too much* or *I don't want you to walk alone at night*, it seems to do something to me, as if they have the ability to make my day instantly better.

Or maybe Luke is just low-key bossy and I like being bossed around by him. I don't have daddy issues, but being a latchkey kid will do that to you.

"Someone's blushing." Zoey's voice causes my head to jerk

up. "Please give me all the juicy details. I need a distraction. How is it with Luke?"

"It's good," I answer, downplaying how happy I am. She doesn't need me to rub my honeymoon stage in her face. "He's picking me up from work tonight."

"You guys have been slowly upping the PDA. Autumn is pissed."

"Tell me something new." I roll my eyes. This is another reason why our group is gradually splitting in two. Autumn and Kai are good friends, and she makes it a point to show up whenever she can, probably to be in Luke's vicinity, but mostly to sneer every time she sees Luke showing me a hint of affection. It's not even that much, since Luke is not the type of guy to rub his relationship in front of other people, but she's making me hesitant to return his touches or kisses. I swear I see her smile every time I flinch or look at her. I overheard her once refer to me as Luke's sister who dated his dead cousin. *True, but still...*

You're just jealous, Gigi. Calm your tits.

"I'm not saying this because I'm jaded right now, but I'm a little worried about you, babe."

"I'm happy, Zoey. Promise."

"It's just," my best friend says before pausing. "This thing with Luke has the potential to blow up. I'd hate to see you get hurt. I was there, you know? When everything happened with Andrew. I saw everything in real time. You've come a long way, Gigi."

"I know." I feel my face soften at the memory of Zoey comforting me when I just found out about Andrew. "Thanks for everything. I owe you so much."

"Just be careful, okay? I don't want to see you that broken again."

I guess she's giving me some tough love, too.

CHAPTER 28

Luke

BEGINNING OF JUNIOR YEAR

AUNT JUDITH

> We missed you last Sunday at church! Andrew has your package. Kisses.

Closing my messenger, I take a quick glimpse at the time displayed on top of my screen. 8:00 p.m. Not too late to stop by at Andrew's dorm first and grab the drawings and little nick knacks Becca makes me every weekend. *I really hope he's alone right now. I don't want to have to see Gigi. That girl just talks and talks and talks.*

I scroll down until I find my cousin's name and shoot him a text.

> Yo, you in your room? Your mom says you have something for me.

An hour goes by and my phone hasn't dinged since I sent Andrew a message. As I pack my laptop in my backpack, I decide to just take my chances and head over to his building.

It's on my way to the parking lot anyway. If I'm lucky, he'll be in his room minus his girlfriend and maybe the two of us can hang out, just the two of us. Like old times.

The second I step out of the library, my pace quickens. I feel the excitement bouncing off my steps as I make my way to where Andrew lives now. I still can't believe that our places are fifteen minutes away from each other. We've never lived this close before. This is going to be the start of a new era, I feel it in my fucking bones. I can already picture us as close as we were before.

For the past year and a half, the moment Andrew and Gigi became official, we started hanging out less and less. A part of me is bitter that he rarely shows up to church anymore, but another part of me gets it. That dude is in love. I've never been in love, but if I were him, maybe I'd skip hanging out with my family too so that I can be Siamese twins with my girlfriend. I just wish he picked out a different one for himself.

My phone rings and sure enough, it's him.

"You home?" I ask. Andrew doesn't answer, and from my end, I can only hear heavy breathing. *Did he seriously butt dial me?* "I'm head—" Before I can finish my sentence, he hangs up. I laugh to myself as I shake my head. *Fucking weirdo.*

The Westgate hall is right in front of me. Above the glass front door, the second window of the third floor is ajar. I think that's his room, but I'm not too sure. I'm bad with layouts, but I'm pretty sure it's that one since I helped him move in two weeks ago. We've only met one other time since he was busy with orientation and Gigi, and I had to wrap up my summer internship. To cancel last Sunday was tempting, just so I could make the drive with Andrew back to his town and meet Becca at church, but the company threw a farewell barbecue for the interns.

Seeing smoke coming out of the space, I'm 100 percent sure it's his room. I chuckle to myself, taking a mental note to call him out on it and tell him to smoke his blunt outside next time. I bet he doesn't know that when the faculty renovated his building last year, they also installed CCTV cameras pointing directly at his window.

I'm downstairs.

Putting a hand on my hip, I feel frustration slowly building inside of me. I'm not mad, not really. I'm just really excited to see Andrew. When I see a guy walk out of the entrance, I jog over so that I can let myself in and not wait for Andrew to reply or call me again.

"Dude, it's me," I say, my voice raised since my knocks are going unanswered, despite the fact that I heard a thud when I first got here. Fifteen minutes pass by before I roll my eyes in defeat. "Whatever," I mutter to myself, making my way back downstairs. *Maybe he's wearing headphones or maybe Gigi is in there and they're fucking.*

I'm playing a video of Gigi at a pizza parlor with her roommate that popped up on my Instagram feed when I bump into white Converse sneakers and a dark pair of jeans.

"Sorry, man," the masculine voice booms.

Taking my eyes off my screen, I spot a familiar figure in front of me. "Hey, Darryl, right?" I ask, not being able to hide the giddiness that's slowly coming back in my voice. *Must be my lucky day.* "Luke. Andrew's cousin? You've met me. We played a round of Fifa together?"

"Oh, yeah." He gives me fist bump as he grins. "What's up?"

"You going to your room?"

"Nope, I'm going to chill out with a buddy of mine."

"Would you mind giving me the passcode?" I ask, resting my hand on the back of my head. "I'm here for Andrew, but he's high off his ass, I think."

Darryl chuckles to himself. "Dude, being high off his ass is probably good for him. Your cousin is intense." I feel my eyebrows scrunching. Andrew and intense are not two words that should go together in a sentence. Slapping my back with a palm, Darryl walks out of the building. "It's nine-nine-two-seven. Catch you later, maybe."

Through the red and blue lights beaming, I can see her. Her hair is wild and her makeup smeared from the tears that are falling freely from her face like a waterfall. I have never once seen Giuliana Bankowski cry. But there she is, the girl that's usually sunshine and rainbows. The girl who likes to post videos on social media narrating every single mundane thing like it's the most important thing on Earth, all tattered and coming undone.

"Luke!" she screams out my name in wails.

"Luke! Tell me it's all a big misunderstanding!" she wails like somehow, if she says it enough times, it will come true.

Knowing Andrew would probably want me to do this, I take four defeated steps toward her, parting the crowd of students whispering and taking goddamn pictures of the yellow tape in front of the entrance. Of the ambulance that just drove away to the morgue. Of the two police cars parked right at the foot of the building.

I pull a screaming Gigi closer to me. We weren't close enough for a tight hug, so I snaked one arm around her, feeling wetness on my shirt. "Uncle Mike is on his way. You can ride with me if you want," I offer, knowing she doesn't have a car.

"May...maybe you're mistaken," she says, her body shaking. "Luke, he wouldn't." Again, she repeats the words like somehow it will make this any different.

"Gi..." I pause. What can I say? "I saw him."

"How?"

"You don't want to know that," I whisper, feeling my own eyes pricking.

"Please, Luke," she begs. "I need to know. Otherwise I'm going to think he's going to walk out of there and laugh, saying he pulled a prank on us." The sound of Gigi's voice cuts through my bones. She might not be my favorite person, but I feel my fist clenching. It's fucked up, I know, but I'm furious at Andrew right now. As furious as I can be at someone. I remember when I was a carefree twelve-year-old. This shit that he just did will do a number on her, no doubt.

"You sure?" Gigi nods frantically. I let her go so I can use my hand to scrub my face, bracing myself for what's to come. "He hung himself. I'm really sorry."

Gigi crouches on the ground. Her screams are causing people to shift their focus on her. I'm about to scream at the group of girls pulling out their phones to take a picture of Gigi, but luckily, Kai, who saw me puke next to the tree half an hour ago after calling the police, my uncle, and Gigi, is already yelling at them to fuck off.

I hear her breathing become erratic. Gigi is clawing at her neck, the tears in her eyes now replaced with panic. I know that look well. I've experienced it before. Had I not been trained exactly for this moment eight years ago, I would probably be next to her doing the same fucking thing.

A memory of what Aunt Judith did for me at my family's funeral when I had my first panic attack flashes in my mind.

"Your mother told me about this beach she went to once. Cape Charles, I think. She said it was her favorite place in the world. She also loved the park next to her office, doesn't she? She always took her lunch break there." I want to tell my aunt to stop, but the words are not leaving my mouth. It feels like a ball of cotton is lodged in my throat. Massaging my shoulder, she

looks at the gravestones in front of us. "Think of happy thoughts, Luke. Picture the beach. Picture the park. Picture a happy memory with her. You got this, honey. I know it's hard, but you got this."

"Whatever picture you have in your head of him right now, replace it, Gi." It's like she doesn't even know I'm here, so I put my palm on her back.

"Think of happy thoughts, Gigi. Picture the ocean. Picture the park. Picture Andrew when you two were together. Happy."

CHAPTER 29
Gigi

STRETCHING OUT MY ARMS, I LET OUT A YAWN. Finals week is coming up and me, Luke, Zoey, and Kai have all been isolating ourselves in Luke and Kai's apartment, pulling all-night study sessions. It's nine o'clock at night and I'm barely holding on. My eyes are droopy, and I feel tingles on my legs from sitting cross-legged next to the coffee table for too long.

"I'm going to take a power nap," I announce.

Without missing a beat, Luke moves his feet and starts walking into his room. Trailing behind him, I find my boyfriend pulling a clean pair of sweatpants from his drawer. "So you're comfy," he says before kissing my head and walking back into the living room to return to his laptop.

My heart warms at how thoughtful he is. Luke is a great boyfriend, a wonderful one, even. He isn't overly affectionate. He doesn't encourage me to do crazy things and he's completely okay with being on the sidelines, letting me have the attention when we are with other people. Not that he has to, because how he is has actually been growing on me, but he makes up for all of those things with acts of kindness, his gentleness that I'm finally getting a taste of, and zero mind games.

Feeling my eyelids getting heavy, I fall asleep with the realization that I might be in love with Lucas Palmer.

❧

I wake up to find a sitting Luke scrolling through his phone, leaning against the headboard. When he notices me stir, his mouth forms a lazy smile.

"Your power nap turned into a two hour long one," he tells me. "Kai and Zoey are in his room."

"Why didn't you wake me?" I ask, not meaning a single word.

"Seems like you needed it, Gi." Pulling me closer to him, he gives me a kiss on the forehead before showing me the screen of his phone. "Are you still going to New York for summer break?"

"Dad offered to pay for my tickets this time, but I don't know yet. Mom has been begging me to come to Kinsdale Springs."

A crease forms on his forehead as he looks at me. "Didn't you say last-minute tickets were expensive?"

"That's why he offered to pay." I shoot Luke a guilty smile. This will be my first summer since everything happened. I've been losing sleep, mulling over what I should do. Although my trip back to Kinsdale Springs is probably long overdue, I don't know if I'm ready yet. But visiting my dad again would piss Mom off and make her feel second best. I guess with all the thinking I forgot that the end of the semester is just around the corner. "You're going back home, right? You promised Becca last week that you would."

Then there's also that. Being a couple at school is one thing, but if I visit Mom, how on Earth are we going to navigate that? As if Luke read my mind, he shoves his phone closer to me so I can read what's on it properly. Luke and I have never even spent our vacations together, with me usually in New York. Andrew used to call those months his Luke and Andrew bonding time.

"Old family friends of mine are getting married in July. I thought we could go together."

"Like a—"

"Yeah," he answers, nervousness dancing in his eyes. "Like a plus-one kind of situation."

Well, holy shit. "Will Andrew's parents be there?" I ask hesitantly.

Luke gives me a casual shrug. "Probably."

"Don't you think it's weird?"

"What's weird?" he asks as he wraps an arm around my stomach and kisses my shoulder. "We started sleeping together in March, Gi. It's time, don't you think? It'll be worse if we drag it on for long. They'll think we're sneaking around."

It is time. I know this. Especially because what Luke and I share, it feels real. A little fucked up, maybe. But it's raw, and simple, and real.

"What's the plan? To just show up and hold hands, hoping they'll get the hint?"

Luke chuckles as he nuzzles my neck, the vibration traveling down my spine. "Hear me out. What if we both go back to Kinsdale Springs after finals? We can ease everyone into it and break the news to the family before the wedding. Your mom and my dad first, and then I don't know...we'll drive over to Uncle Mike and Aunt Judith and tell them the news. Over lunch or something."

"Just so you know, your aunt doesn't like me," I sigh, already dreading the conversation.

"That's a load of crap. Everyone likes you."

"Except for her."

Luke gives me a look, trying to communicate *be serious* with his eyes. "Well, she never said anything to me about it."

"Because she thinks we're not close," I say, causing him to laugh. "It's not bullshit, Luke. Andrew was partying nonstop his senior year. She told him I was corrupting him. He told me himself."

Luke snorts in response. "Andrew started drinking when he was fifteen. He probably just stopped caring about hiding it."

"Yeah, but she doesn't know that. She thinks I corrupted her precious altar boy."

"Altar boys are only for Catholics, Gi. We don't have them."

"Says the guy with a tattoo of a saint." I roll my eyes. "You also don't have those."

"He was a disciple first, smartass."

We both laugh and my heart tingles, realizing that conversations about Andrew don't make the both of us flinch anymore. He will always be a part of us, good and bad. That's the thing about losing someone, isn't it? At some point, you have no choice but to move forward.

"She'll learn to love you. I'm pretty sure."

"How can you be sure?" I still remember the side-eye she used to give me.

Luke pauses for a moment. I'm trying to figure out how he's going to defend that lie of his, but then he surprises me with his answer. "Because she'll see that I'm happy when I'm with you."

"Then I'll come," I say, planting my smiling lips on his chest. This is important for him. Besides, how can I say no to that adorable face of his? Filled with hope. "Let's go back to Kinsdale Springs for the summer." *I'm happy, too, probably the happiest I've ever been in a long time.*

CHAPTER 30
Luke

LEANING ON THE DOORJAMB, MY FOCUS immediately goes to the two giant suitcases and the duffel bag Gigi is desperately trying to zip shut. "Gi, you do know we have a washing machine at home, right?" I tease, trying to hide my smirk under my baseball cap.

"I know, I know," she answers, finally succeeding with the zipper. Gigi paces around the room, packing her things one by one inside her backpack. "But I haven't been back in a while, and I don't like half of these clothes anymore. I might just leave them at home." She opens one of her suitcases and pulls out a few T-shirts with prints on them. "I thought about selling them online or throwing them away, but I thought maybe Becca might want them. She's still too small for them now, but maybe in a year or two, you know?"

Chuckling, I bounce myself off the door and help her refold the shirts. "You're rambling."

"I'm sorry," she says, grimacing. "I do that sometimes."

"You haven't done it in a while." Giving her a kiss on the head, I pull her closer by the waist, trying to remember the last time she was like this—a ball of excited energy. This used to be her standard setting. It still was when she arrived on campus a year ago.

"Are you annoyed?" There is uncertainty infused in her tone.

Old me, the one who didn't spend every waking second thinking about this girl, would answer yes to this question without hesitation. Gigi was everything I wasn't. A part of me wonders now whether I was just jealous of her, that she was so carefree because life hadn't dealt her a bad hand.

"Don't be stupid," I tell her the truth. "You never annoy me."

We both laugh. Life is funny like that. One day I hate her for invading my life, the next she has me wrapped around her pinky finger. Aside from Becca, nobody has had this much control over me. Thinking of Becca makes me remember how much I loathed her when she was born. Maybe I have a pattern.

"Let me pee, and then we can go." Gigi lets go of me and I use the time to check my phone. One message from Kai, one message from a group chat with all of the scholarship recipients courtesy of the Daedalus Foundation, and one more from Dad.

DAD

> Bianca told me you and Gigi are coming home today. I'll be back Sunday next week. Doing a Highlights of the Midwest Tour right now.

Most days, I still don't know what to say to him. He seems to be sober, from the limited interactions I have when I'm home. Even if I wanted to and went back to Kinsdale Springs more often, I still would not see a lot of Dad. Not that I want to. I've seen more of him than other sons have their fathers. I've seen him telling me everything was my fault, I've seen him buck naked covered in his own puke, and I've seen him sobbing to a picture of his dead wife.

Ok. See you then.

He's always out driving multi-day tours now that Becca is older and he has Bianca. At least according to Becca, he's good to her. That's enough for me not to cut him out completely out of my life.

"You ready?" Gigi's voice has me lifting my head up.

"Of course."

"How are we going to play this?" Gigi asks me, half an hour into the drive.

"Play what?"

"Breaking the news."

"I haven't really thought about it." There's no YouTube video teaching you how to tell your family that you're dating your stepsister. "My dad isn't home, though. Do you think we should wait until he's back?"

"When will he be back?"

"Sunday next week."

"That's kind of perfect," Gigi says. "Maybe we can tell Andrew's parents first."

It's not a bad idea, to be honest. Knowing Bianca and my dad, I don't think they will care so much that we're together. Bianca might be a loose cannon on this one, but Dad won't give a shit. Besides, my aunt and uncle's stamp of approval is more important to me than the two of them. They have been there ever since my mom died. Aunt Judith went to more PTA meetings for me and Becca than Dad ever did when I was still living at home.

Taking her hand in mine, I feel the coat of wetness on her palm. “You nervous?”

“Yeah, I am,” she admits. “I think you’re a little crazy to think everything will work out for us so easily.”

I feel my back go rigid at her words. “Hey, Gi. If you’re having second thoughts and you don’t want to do this—”

“Oh, shut up.” She doesn’t let me finish. “I love being with you. You know I’m all in. I just hope for your sake everything will work out fine.” *She loves being with you. She’s all in.* Her words cause a ripple of heat to buzz through my core. This must be what it feels like. To not be someone’s second choice.

When I see the sign *Kinsdale Springs* on the side of the road, I say a silent prayer. But not to God, I haven’t done that in years.

Hey, Andrew, if you can listen to me, ask the big man to make sure everything goes smoothly, yeah? I’ll forgive you for leaving if you do this for me.

CHAPTER 31

Gigi

It's past dinner time when we arrive. Mom made it a point to take the day off today, something she never does. From the window, I can see her and Becca peering outside. They must have waited for us. The moment Luke stops the engine, the front door swings open and I see my mother running out, followed by my stepsister.

"*Piccola mia*!" She rushes to me with her arms open. "You're here."

Her generously sized boobs are crushing mine, suffocating me. I don't care. I miss her. "Hi, Mom," I say with a giggle. When I open my eyes, I see Luke give Becca an elaborate, secret handshake, his expression proud and his smile genuine.

My mom lets go of me and goes over to Luke while Becca does the opposite. The last time I saw this little princess was at Andrew's funeral last September.

"Hey, little one," I hum my pet name for her. "Look at you getting taller." I rough up her hair as guilt creeps up on me. If Luke has really been visiting her regularly, which I know he does since he has invited me from time to time, but I always decline out of fear of Andrew's parents reacting to us being an item, that means I am the only one who hasn't been meeting her. I hope she understands my reasoning behind it.

"Miss you, Gigi," she says, smiling as she gives me a half hug. "Bianca! I owe you a donut!"

"Why do you owe Mom a donut?" I ask curiously.

"Oh, it's nothing." My mom waves her hand around, her smile suspicious.

"I was so sure that you two would come here fighting, that we made a bet." Becca gives me a smirk that's all mischief. "He doesn't like you very much, you know."

Luke throws his head back and bursts out laughing. "I told you already. I changed my opinion; she's cool." He's talking to her, but he's winking at me, causing my stomach to do somersaults.

It's crazy to think that all of my Luke memories attached to this house only consist of him either arriving home, or leaving home. With him only coming back in the summer when I was all the way in another state, we never really did anything together. This summer will be different, and I'm all here for it. I can feel it. New memories and all that.

My eyes widen when I see what these two did. In the living room, a big banner saying *Welcome Home* hangs on the wall. Typical of her. Although she works a lot, when it comes down to it, she's a soccer mom, through and through. I bet she knew that this homecoming is different for me and Luke because of what happened.

"My heart is so full," my mother says, clutching her chest. "All the children together under one roof. Once Vince is back, our family will be complete." I swallow the bile rising up my throat at her remark. Yeah, telling Andrew's parents is daunting, but it's a necessary evil. Luke was right, the longer we keep this a secret, the more ridiculous the situation becomes.

From the corner of my eye, I see Luke tensing at the mention of his father. I wonder what happened between them. Although I managed to coax a shitload of information from Luke about him, which is a miracle in itself, he rarely talks about Vince. Never Vince. In fact, he always redirects the conversation every time his father comes up in a conversation.

Five minutes after excusing myself to go on a much-needed pee break, I frown when I see what's happening in the living room. My mom is putting a fitted sheet on the air mattress and Luke has his bag set up in the living room.

"Why isn't this set up in Becca's room?" I ask. "And Luke, I thought we agreed that I would sleep with her?"

He shrugs. "It's fine," is all he says.

My mom looks at me with an uncertain smile. "Becca is a little too old for sharing, Gigi. She even has a sign taped to her door upstairs that no other people are allowed in her room."

"She won't mind," I try to argue. I'm not letting Luke sleep with zero privacy in his own house. "Let me talk to her about it." She might be at the age where she thinks boys have cooties, even her brother, but she adores me.

"It's fine," Luke repeats himself.

"Then let me have the air mattress," I say.

"Well, Luke and I talked about it. We think it would be best if you sleep in your own room."

I cock my eyebrow, about to argue with my mom, but then Luke repeats himself again for the third time. "Gi, seriously. No big deal. Go up, shower, and get some rest."

My mom looks at Luke and then to me. Her mother's intuition must be off the charts because her eyes start narrowing and I can tell she senses something between us. She doesn't say anything though, and I'm not about to open that can of worms within an hour of being back in Kinsdale Springs.

CHAPTER 32
Luke

Every time I come home, one thing always comes to mind during my first night—I miss my old life.

Not the one after the fire, but the one from before. The one where we haven't moved to Kinsdale Springs yet because even though we didn't live in a mansion, we had everything we needed. The one where Dad was gone a lot, but he was still a father figure. The one where we had big family gatherings, my mother was still alive, and my biggest problem was a baby sister who wouldn't stop crying.

Now, I only see my relatives when I go to church at Marble Crest instead of at family barbecues. Although the building that burned down was able to be renovated, the graveyard next to it serves as a reminder that almost all the Palmers died that day.

Closing my eyes shut, I try my best to let the anger leave my body. I toss and turn when I realize that nothing is working. My family's ghosts are not leaving me tonight, and one in particular is haunting me with every force imaginable. The one with the newest tombstone.

Before I even register what I'm doing, I'm walking up the

dark staircase. Snores from Bianca and Dad's room can be heard and I breathe a little better. When I see warm light seeping through under the door of my old room, I open it without knocking.

"Can't sleep?" I ask without looking at Gigi, closing the door and locking it.

"Nope," she says, her voice breaking. When I turn around, I find my girlfriend trying her best to get out of the fetal position she's in.

"You're thinking about him, huh?"

Gigi's eyes widen before looking away. "I didn't w—"

Sighing, I turn the light switch off, turning the whole room pitch black. "It's your first time back, Gi," I say as I pull the covers and join her on the bed. "You're allowed to think about him."

I lay next to her with one hand under my head and the other one in my pocket. The ceiling looks dark from down here, different from my childhood bedroom where Andrew and I jumped around and stuck glow-in-the-dark dinosaur stickers all over the room.

Gigi scoots closer to me, her fingers going through my hair that definitely needs some trimming. I haven't let them get cut ever since she told me she prefers my hair a little longer over my old go-to buzz cut. I take her hand in mine and pull her closer to me.

"You probably know about the fire," I say, trying to keep my voice calm despite the panic brewing inside of me. I've never told anyone about this. It was a need-to-know basis, and the ones who knew didn't find out because I had a heart-to-heart session with them. "My dad drank a lot after that. He needed an outlet, I guess. He stopped the drinking at some point, but he didn't like it every time I brought up our relatives. A part of me hates him for being absent, but another part of me gets it. He wants to block the noise out. I know because they're always there, in the back of my mind. Andrew and I used to visit their graves all the time, but he isn't here this time around and Becca doesn't remember them." I feel wetness on the crook of my neck where her face is resting. "I'm not telling you this so that you feel sorry for me, Gi. I'm telling you this because it's normal for you to think about him." Ignoring the stabbing pain in my chest, I press my lips to the tip of her nose and close my eyes. "Blocking things out won't solve your problems. I'd rather have you tell me that you're thinking about him than you becoming my father."

"Will you tell me about them?" she asks softly, surprising me. "What they were like?"

"You really want to know about my family?" I lift my head up, disbelieving. People usually just try to pump me out for juicy fucking details about the fire. Gossipers are the reason why I only talked to Andrew about the Palmers.

"I do."

"Aunt Vanessa was Dad's twin. I used to call her twin daughters spawns of Satan." *Sweet little Cathleen and Mary.* "She was the only girl in the family. The rest were sons. They were all younger than Dad, so their children were younger than me." *All still in primary school.* "Uncle Mike was an only child, so Andrew didn't have any first cousins." I swallow the lump in my throat before continuing. "I don't think I've ever told you about Mom. The whole family didn't really like her because she thinks churches are overt cults." Blowing out a breath, I feel my heart hammering in my chest. "She was so pretty, Gi. Becca looks just like her."

"You're okay, Luke. Think of happy thoughts," she whispers.

Mom reading me a book before bedtime.

"And then there were the grandmas. They were widowed, bored out of their fucking minds. They were also twins, my grandma and Andrew's. They used to dress us up in matching outfits and pretend that we were twins, too. It was insane. I think they were just looking for attention. Two similar-looking little boys with two identical grandmas." I chuckle at the memory of the four of us eating ice cream together most Sundays. *Fuck.* I lift my other arm that's not hugging Gigi, resting the palm of my hand on my eyes. "I loved them all, Gi." A confession years too fucking late. If I had a chance to see each and every one of them again, I would tell them.

Think of happy thoughts, Luke.

But nobody is lucky enough to be able to speak to the dead, so I rasp out the words to the one that's still breathing instead. The one person who's been hijacking my brain when I try to think of happy thoughts. "I love you."

Gigi stiffens in my arms. I kiss her forehead to calm her down. "I'm not even going to fucking pretend that I'm not a consolation prize. If Andrew were here, it would be him on this bed instead of me. But I can't help how I feel. You don't have to say it back." I don't need to hear it, I just need her to goddamn know. Nobody knows what's going to happen tomorrow.

"I love you. I'm falling so hard the thought of you leaving me one day scares me." With the moonlight shining through the window, I can see that her eyes are glassy. "And I think," she drawls out her words in whispers and then pauses, her breath shaky. "You're nobody's consolation prize, Luke."

When she kisses me, I feel the smile on her face that makes me almost believe her.

CHAPTER 33
Gigi

EIGHTEEN YEARS OLD

"I don't get it," Andrew scoffs, shaking his head. He is smiling, but he's anything but happy. "Why won't you say it back?"

I almost laugh in disbelief, but doing that would cause us to fight again, and that's something I'm just not going to waste my energy on. We closed that fucking chapter. Shut. There's no need to rehash old wounds. "I'm just not ready yet."

"We've been going out for a long time, babe." When I don't answer, he places his elbow on his knees, his eyes looking to the floor, solemn. "Is it because I cheated?"

The thing is, I know he regrets it. I believe Andrew when he said that it was a one-time thing. Once a cheater always a cheater doesn't really apply to him, at least I don't think so. Andrew was a mess after it happened. He even stopped going to church with his parents altogether so that he didn't have to see her. It didn't matter if they were angry or we were already meeting the other six days of the week, despite not even living in the same town. People who don't feel guilty don't do that.

Guys who plan on cheating again also don't give their girlfriends full access to their phones and laptops. In one of his apology letters, I even got a sticky note with all of his passwords—his school email, cash apps, and streaming accounts included.

"No," I answer, grinding my molars. "It's because you won't tell me the reason why you cheated."

"Giuliana," he says my name half pleading, half in a warning tone. I start feeling the anger come back. *I'm Giuliana now.*

"Just tell me the truth. I don't get you. You don't go from planning your first fuck with your girlfriend to banging someone else without a reason."

"We've been over this, Gigi." He pins me down with an exasperated stare. "I thought we were done with this."

"Well, you brought it up."

Andrew sighs. His hand runs through the dirty blond waves of his hair. "Me telling you wouldn't do us any fucking good."

Why can't he see that him not *telling me is also not doing us any good?*

Fighting the tears that are about to break free, I look up to the ceiling. "Take me home, please. I don't want to be here anymore."

"Gigi." Again, my name comes in a half-pleading, half-warning tone. He wants me to drop this. I think it's unfair that he wants all of me, all my love, but I can't get all of him. I accept the cheating. I accept the slip-up. I just want to know why.

"Don't *Gigi* me," I say, seething.

"I love you," he dares to say. "Don't say it back. Say it back. You know I do."

And I hate that I know it's true. But I can't speak the words and give myself fully unless I know. "If you really love me, then tell me the truth," I beg, hoping this one will finally do the trick. "I need to know why you chose Rachel instead of me. I need to know why you chose to lose your virginity in some bathroom at a fucking house party."

"Don't push me, Gigi. You don't know anything about anything!" His blue eyes turn icy, and I feel the hair on the nape of my neck stand up. Yelling is not something that we do to each other. He's been like this lately. Dr. Jekyll and Mr. Hyde. Even before Rachel. If he wasn't pleading his case every second of every day, I'd think he was going to dump me.

"Take me the fuck home." I try to keep my voice stern, but inside my brain is scrambled.

"You want to know why I did it?" There's no stopping him now. "Because I was drunk. Because you weren't there." Andrew's eyes meet mine, and this time they're glossy. "I was fucking stupid. And believe me, I know I messed up," Andrew sobs. The sounds coming out of his mouth splinter my heart more than his confession. "I'm sorry."

CHAPTER 34

Luke

"OH COME ON!" GIGI ROLLS HER EYES, GRINNING. "Just tell me what Kai said to you. I promise I won't tell Zoey."

Shaking my head, I drive through the patches of land separating the town we just passed and Marble Crest. "I'm not going to tell you, Gi. You're asking me in her place. Don't deny it."

"But they need help. They're both not communicating properly." I sense genuine concern in her voice, but nope. I'm not going to budge.

"Be that as it may, I'm not going to betray my friend's trust."

"Not even for me?" Gigi turns her back toward the car door so that she's facing me. With her arms crossed over her chest, she fake pouts. *Cute*.

"Not even for you." I smile, putting a hand on her thigh.

The truth is, before we left for summer vacation, Kai told me he was going to see where his relationship goes until the end of senior year. If all goes well, he's planning on proposing to her before he leaves Ravensfield. I didn't need to tell him twice that his relationship is on its last legs, but the dude is a fucking romantic and he's in love. He thinks putting a ring on it will fix whatever issues they have. *Not my circus, not my monkeys.*

"Your loyalty to him is irritating," Gigi groans. "I'm just trying to help them, Luke. Our friends."

"And the last time I checked, you're not a therapist yet."

"You are mean," she says with no bite, all smiles. "I hate you."

"No, you don't." I bark out a laugh as I make the turn to Aunt Judith and Uncle Mike's street. "You love me, remember?"

I love you. I'm falling so hard the thought of you leaving me one day scares me.

You're nobody's consolation prize, Luke.

Pretty words tied together. It meant everything to me when she said that last night. A wake-up call. A promise. Proof that I'm good enough as I am.

"And you love me." Gigi moves closer to the driver's seat, planting a kiss on my cheek. "Which is why you're going to help me help Kai and Zoey, by telling me what he said."

With her mouth still on my skin, I kill the engine and turn my head around. I taste the lipstick that she put on as war paint for today and lick it off my bottom lip. "Nice try, Gigi. But the answer is still no. Now, let's go in before they spot us like this."

"Honey, we've missed you!" Aunt Judith's arms wrap me with all the love she has to give, but barely anyone to give it to. "We haven't seen you in a month."

I scratch my head as I swallow the guilt that's coming in ripples. I've been spending a lot of time with Gigi. That, coupled with finals, I just didn't have the fucking energy to make the drive. Four hours in total for a day trip felt too long when I could be using the time either at the library or balls deep in my girlfriend. I get it now. Why Andrew was so enamored with her. She makes you feel like every waking moment you're not spending with her is a moment wasted.

"Hey, Aunt Judith." Roscoe, their poodle, is already humping my right leg. "Exam week was crazy. Sorry we couldn't make it here sooner."

"Well, you're here now, Lucas." Aunt Judith's eyes move from me to the person next to me. Gigi waves her hands as she stands, giving her an awkward smile. "Gigi, it's been a while. How are you?" my aunt asks before pulling Gigi into a hug. Relief washes over me when I realize Gigi was probably just overthinking when she said Aunt Judith doesn't like her. She's all smiles and giggles.

When we find my uncle in the kitchen, I feel my throat drying. I came here with a plan—to tell them about me and Gigi. I thought for sure that everything would go well. But behind my uncle is a wall filled with pictures of their most cherished treasure. Their one and only son.

What if they think I stole Gigi from him? What if they think I'm sick in the fucking head? Nobody had a problem with her dating her step-second cousin, but her stepbrother? For fuck's sake, they're as religious as Jesus himself. I don't think the Bible condones what we're doing.

I feel like I'm getting hit by a freight train as reality hits me from all angles. Uncle Mike is proudly talking about his mission trip to Ecuador, but my brain is processing the fact that I might get disowned when I leave this house. *How did you think this could possibly go well for you, Luke?* Back at Ravensfield, it was so easy to pretend as if we were just two normal people falling in love. Here? I'm the guy who massacred his whole family and is dating his dead second cousin's girlfriend. *His stepsister.*

The moment the coffee hits my system and all the pleasantries have been made, I take a long, deep breath.

"There is something that I need to tell you both." Gigi looks at me in horror. *Was I supposed to give her a heads-up first? Shit, it's too late now.*

"Oh?" Aunt Judith stops munching on her cheesecake. She pauses for a second before breaking out into a smile. "Did you decide to apply for a master's degree?"

Shaking my head, I give her a tight-lipped smile. "No. Not that, I'm afraid."

Giving Gigi one last look, I try to remember everything that makes coming clean to them worth it. I don't want to keep her as a dirty little secret. I don't want to cheapen what we have. My heart sinks when I realize the only person who would probably understand this, the only one who would probably support me from the get-go, would be Andrew.

"What is it then, Luke?" My uncle's stern, but kind voice pulls me back to reality. He's probably wondering why I brought my stepsister along with me when I usually come alone.

I'm dating your dead son's girlfriend. I'm in a relationship with my stepsister. Mulling over what I should say, I go with the best option possible. The truth. "I'm in love with Gigi."

"This Gigi?" Aunt Judith asks, pointing her finger to my girlfriend. Next to me, Gigi just stays quiet and meek. I've never seen her so still in my life. My uncle mirrors Gigi's demeanor, except the color in his face is gone.

"Yes," I answer with a smile. "This Gigi."

"I...I don't understand." My aunt shakes her head in disbelief. "When did this happen? I thought you two weren't even friends?"

"We started seeing each other during spring break," I say,

leaving out the details of our origin story. Knowing full well that even though Uncle Mike is known for being a cool and chill pastor, he's not going to appreciate me admitting that I took Gigi's virginity during a random fuck while drunk off my ass. "I understand if you two are not okay with this, but she makes me very happy."

"You're stepsiblings," my aunt states the obvious.

When I realize Gigi is not going to be a willing participant in this conversation, I answer for us. "Who have never lived under the same roof."

"Mike." His name is an exasperated sigh. A request for her husband to take over and start giving us lectures about how wrong and sinful this is.

Just when I thought Uncle Mike was about to tell us that we are going to hell, he opens his mouth. "I'm glad you two found each other."

CHAPTER 35
Gigi

Maybe Luke's negative Nancy attitude is rubbing off on me, but I can't shake the feeling that everything is not supposed to be this simple. Call it intuition or whatever, but the way Andrew's parents gave us their blessing yesterday? Something's not right. They should be pissed, right? They should want to disown Luke. Andrew's mom was about to say something, I sensed it, but when her husband all but gave us his thumbs up, she stayed quiet real quick. *Or maybe they really are nice people and Luke is right. They like seeing him happy.*

Whatever qualms I have, Luke is not sharing it. He's like a whole new person with less chinks in his armor.

"I can't wait to get back to campus," Luke rasps, his sweaty hands firm on my hips. Without looking at him, I know he's wearing a smile on his face. "I miss loud sex."

I want to laugh, but the sound gets replaced by a whimper that I muffle with my palm instead when his thrusts go harder inside me, pushing my head further down to the pillow. *Fuck, is doggy style supposed to feel this good? Can he see my butthole from this angle?*

"Yeah." He chuckles as he pants, light and carefree. Like he has a new lease on life. "I can see it from here, Gi."

Fuck. "I just said it out loud, didn't I?"

Flipping me over, as if saving me from further embarrassment, he lays me on my back as he pushes himself inside me again. This time it's slower, more deliberate. His face is directly over mine and I can't help but run my hands through his messy hair. Our eyes meet and the honey color softens, turning my insides liquid.

"I love you, Gigi," he says, his breaths labored. "I can't wait to meet your friends tomorrow." I feel him hitting the tender spot deep inside me. "I can't wait to tell our parents." I feel the friction on my inside walls as he drags himself out of me lazily. "This is it, Gi." I feel him plunge into me again. "We're really happening." I feel his dick pulsating as he releases his cum.

Still connected, Luke tucks a loose hair strand behind my ear. The man on top of me is not the same brooding boy who started a hate campaign against me when he begrudgingly had to give up his room for me. He's chatty, cracking jokes. Luke has changed and he's healing.

Swallowing the lump in my throat, I make my decision. I'm choosing to keep my doubts about Andrew's parents and their dubious approval to myself. A smiling, happy Lucas Palmer is such a precious sight to see; I don't want to bring him down from his high.

"You are the best thing that ever happened to me. Do you know that?" he tells me before putting his soft lips on mine. I feel honored to be on the receiving end of all of Luke's love. Since he doesn't hand it out for free, you know that it's the real deal. And in a sea of fakeness and fleeting connections, this man is a needle in a haystack. A rarity in a generation of men who'd tell you sweet nothings, only to leave you the next day for someone else.

"You are the best thing that ever happened to me," I whisper. I feel the stinging in my eyes. I don't know why I'm about to cry, I just am. Everything is so good, and overwhelming, and beautifully painful at the same time. "Do you know that, Luke?" My hands cup his cheek as I kiss him with all the love I have for him, and I feel him hardening again inside me. "You're always going to be my first choice," I say, bringing our foreheads together.

Although it was one painful journey to get here, I can't help but think that everything played out how it was supposed to be. God's plan, if you will. Life works in mysterious ways, and you can't know what's in store for you. If Lucas Palmer is the one who I'm supposed to end up with, to be with for the rest of my life, I will die a happy woman.

"Will you come with me?" he asks as he thrusts himself in and out of me once again. One of his hands is hooking my thigh on his hip while the other one covers my breast, rolling my nipple between his fingers. "After you're done with school? I'll do my master's in Ravensfield and then I want to move, Gi."

If his goal is to manipulate me into saying yes while he fucks me stupid and sends me into a state of delirium with the way his tongue is rolling on my breasts, licking every inch of pebbled skin, then he's succeeding. I want to say yes, but words are not coming out. We have tried sex the rough and hard way, usually during quickies when we're sloshed, but this. The slow, lazy sex with kisses in between. The kind of sex that makes me feel like I'm cherished. This is my fucking kryptonite, and he knows it. So, I nod frantically, chanting my agreement in my head. *Yes. Yes. Yes. Wherever you go. Yes. Take me with you.*

"Would you do that for me?" I want to cry in frustration when he straightens his back, moving his mouth away from my nipples, but then he licks two fingers and touches my throbbing clit, causing my eyes to flutter. "Would you be with me that way?" I want to ask what he means. We're already together. As Luke slides into me again, he makes me understand with words that cause my heart to have its own kind of orgasm. "I want the whole package with you, Gi. I want to take you with me, and then I want marriage. Children. A dog that nobody's going to fucking walk except for me because you and the kids are too lazy to take it out. The whole shebang."

I want to tell Luke that I want that, too. I want to tell him how happy I am that he's opening up to me. I want to tell him that I think he's the strongest, most beautiful person on Earth I have ever met. My thoughts disperse into thin air the moment my climax takes me under and I start trembling.

I'll tell him next time, because with Luke, there is going to be a next time. We're not going anywhere. We're really doing this.

CHAPTER 36
Luke

TAKING OUT MY RIGHT HAND THAT'S SHOVED IN MY jeans' pocket, I reach out to shake the hands of Gigi's high school friends one by one, hoping they don't notice the cold sweat covering my palm. I forgot how popular she was in high school. She was on the cheer team, for fuck's sake. She was the opposite of me. At Ravensfield, if Gigi's not with me, she's mostly with Zoey or Zach. I guess that's what happens when your boyfriend kills himself in his dorm room—you become a social pariah.

"I'm Mackenzie," the girl with the blonde hair says as she squeezes my hand. "My brother used to be in your grade. Noah Baylor?"

"Luke," I answer, nodding. "Yeah, I know him." He used to ask me whether I sold weed or not, as if everyone who's poor deals drugs.

"Lauren," another one introduces herself in a sing-song voice. "I was Gigi's bff in high school."

"Luke."

"I'm Lauren's boyfriend," the tall guy next to her says, offering me a firm grip. "Bryan. Nice to meet you, man."

"Luke." *How many times do I have to say my name tonight?*

The next girl that's standing between Lauren and Gigi reaches her hand out but says nothing. She gawks at me with an uncertain smile, tilting her head to the side. Slowly, she looks at her friends before shaking her head as she apologizes. "Sorry, I didn't mean to stare," Gigi's friend says. "You look so much—" She has the wisdom to cut herself off, but I finish her sentence in my head for her. *You look so much like Andrew.* "I'm Ivy."

"Our grandmas were twins," I offer her an explanation, taking her hand. "Luke."

As I introduce myself for the fourth, fifth, and sixth time, my mind wanders off to a place I promised myself I wouldn't go shortly after I realized I had feelings for Gigi. When there are only two of you left in the family, it's hard not to compare yourself. I thought I was done playing this game when Andrew died, but tonight is proving me wrong.

While I'm sticking out like a sore thumb in this group of former cheerleaders, Bryan is fitting right in. The guy looks like he could be a jock, or at least he belongs to the cool crowd. I bet Andrew had no problem charming their pants off when Gigi introduced them. I bet he did charm their pants off.

"Luke, are you okay?" my girlfriend whispers while her friends are looking at the menu. Her hand slides down to my knee, putting pressure so that I'd stop bobbing it up and down.

"Yeah, why wouldn't I be?"

"Sooo," Lauren coos. "Tell us all the juicy details. How does it feel like to be dating the stepsis?" She giggles. She actually fucking giggles.

"Babe," Bryan warns Lauren, shooting me a sympathetic look. *Should I be calling Gigi babe, too? Did Andrew do it? Does she like to be called babe?*

"What?" Lauren looks at her boyfriend, showing no signs of stopping. "I'm just curious, okay? Gigi doesn't tell me anything. She's all the way in Ravensfield while we're in Texas. I want to hear all the juicy deets." Her eyes dart to me again as she flashes me a big smile. "So, Luke. The floor is yours. Spill."

"It's fine, Lauren. We're happy," Gigi answers for me, saving me the trouble. *Why is her answer like that?* She doesn't sound like someone who's in the best relationship they've ever experienced. Because that's how I feel. I don't know what I would've said to Lauren, but *it's fine*, would not be fucking it.

The rest of the dinner goes by excruciatingly slowly. Bryan goes out for a smoke and I follow him outside. Not that I need one, but I'm just not used to this. A table full of chatty girls talking about movies, gossip, and the caption of their selfies. I never did this with Autumn. We met in college, so all her friends already knew me. Since our relationship was already on a downward spiral after the weekend I met her parents, I never met her high school crew.

When Gigi told me her friends were back home from college and she would like me to meet them, I was happy. I still am. I guess I'm just not used to this side of Gigi. The cheerleader. The popular girl. The one who mirrors Andrew's high school life so well it hurts my chest just to think about it.

My cousin was all-around perfect. Grandmas and grandpas in his congregation would gush about how he had impeccable manners, clueless to the fact that he was sneaking off to parties at night, while girls would swoon over how cute he was. His teammates, the ones I have met anyway, didn't care about any of that. They, however, respected the hell out of him for being a damn good shooting guard.

The one thing that always made me envious of Andrew was the way he still had an intact family. It would make me so fucking pissed when he told me that he didn't want to spend time with his parents. It drove me wild when he started skipping church when he started dating Gigi. When he completely bailed, I had to find excuses for him to calm his parents down even though he also withdrew from me. The son of the pastor doesn't get to stop coming.

Tonight, I'm starting to realize there is one more point that I should add to the list of things that Andrew is better at than me. Being a part of Gigi's life.

CHAPTER 37
Gigi

HERE GOES NOTHING.

Here goes everything.

"Mom, Vince." I take a calming breath. Three of them, actually. Luke wanted to be the one to break the news to them, as well, just like he did with Andrew's parents, but I said no. Maybe if it comes out of my mouth, it will soften the blow for my mother. Luke's family might be cool Christians with their rock bands and bake sales, but Mom? Despite her getting pregnant with me and the divorce, my mother was raised an old-school Catholic. I'm lucky if she doesn't take out her bottle of holy water and DIY an exorcism here at home. "Maybe you've noticed that ever since Luke and I came back for summer break, we've been close."

"And I'm so happy for you both," my mother gushes. "I was always sad that you were an only child. Now you have a brother and a sister." *Well, shit.*

Scratching my temple, I let out a nervous chuckle. This is not funny. Not fucking funny at all. But I can't stop and Luke is gawking at me like I've gone insane. I clear my throat.

"Uhm, okay, let's start this again," I say, causing everyone to look at me in confusion.

Congratulations, Gigi. You've made it worse.

"Honey, what is going on?" Mom asks. "Can this wait until tomorrow? I'm sure Vince would like to get some rest, and I have to be at the hospital in a few hours."

"Luke and I are together." There. I said it.

Mom's eyebrows reach her forehead. I think she's shell-shocked because she's not saying anything. She doesn't even look disappointed; her face is blank.

A pale Vince is the first one to react. "Together as in a couple?"

"Yes, Dad," Luke answers.

"For how long?"

"Since spring break." I don't miss the different tone Luke is using with his dad in comparison to the one he used with his aunt and uncle. I bite my bottom lip as I think about how this news will probably worsen their already strained relationship. I just want Luke to be happy and I wish I knew how to make this better.

"Your uncle Mike will have something to say about this," Vince grumbles. "They're not going to be happy."

I want to tell Vince that they already know, but Luke beats me to it. "We talked to them first," is all he says. Whatever he wants to do with his career, I hope he's not planning on becoming a diplomat.

Before Luke rattles his father some more, I interject. "Luke and I went to Marble Crest to visit Andrew's grave and to have coffee with them. We decided to break the news to them then. We thought it would be best for them to hear it from us than other people."

"And I'm the last one to know, huh? You're dating my wife's daughter, and I don't even get a phone call first as a common courtesy," Vince huffs as he turns his gaze away from the both of us, looking outside the window. He's not even addressing me. All of his frustration goes to his son. My heart aches for Luke, remembering the story he told me about his childhood.

Earth to Mom? She looks like she might be mute. I think I broke my mother.

Next to me, I feel the tension seeping out of Luke. He pins his father down with a glare but decides to say nothing. Proving my point further that he sucks at diplomacy, Luke opens his mouth. "We don't have that kind of relationship."

Lucas Palmer. Straight shooter. And when he wants to be, mean. I have been on the receiving end of this crap. As much as I think Vince is far from perfect, that must have stung. I don't need to complete my bachelor's in psychology to know that this conversation is not about us dating anymore.

"It's wrong, son," Vince sighs, shaking his head. He gestures his hand toward me before letting out a frustrated exhale. "She's Andrew's girl. Think of what people are going to spread around town." *Stab my heart, why don't you, Vince?*

Luke barks out a bitter laugh. If I didn't know any better, I'd say he's about to kill his father with his bare hands by the way murder is written all over his face. I always thought Luke hated me in the beginning; I was wrong. Luke was only annoyed by my presence. This is what it looks like when Luke despises someone.

"Isn't that rich coming from you, Dad? You're really going to tell me what's wrong and right?" Luke stabs his own chest with his finger as his tone gets angrier and angrier. "*I* should think about what other people are going to say? Really?"

"Luke, calm down," I try to warn him. Defuse the situation. But it falls on deaf ears.

"Look in the goddamn mirror," Luke sneers, completely ignoring me. I don't like the glint I see in his eyes when he turns his head to face my mother. "Does Bianca know about you, Dad?"

I see Vince's face turn a shade of red, exactly like one of those cartoon characters that would have fumes coming out of their ears.

"Luke, don't do this right now," I warn him again, knowing there is only a 2 percent chance he might listen. Luke is on a mission at the moment, and it's to obliterate his father. I can't say I blame him, I just wish my mom was not the collateral damage.

Luke actually turns to me, breaking out of his angry trance. I use the moment to mouth *Think of happy thoughts, Luke* to him. Again, and again, and again until his face softens. He gives me a slight nod before turning to face Vince again. "Accept it, or don't. Do what you want, Dad. You always do, anyway."

I rush to the door when Luke starts marching out of the house like he might catch fire if he stays a minute longer. I catch up to him just as he's yanking his car door open. "Luke, where are you going?"

"I'm going for a drive." Gone is the gentle and loving Lucas Palmer I have gotten to know these past few months. This one in front of me is reminiscent of the Luke from before we were together. Closed off. Brooding.

"Let me come with you," I say, certain that I can make him feel better. He just needs a long hug. Intimacy.

"No." He must notice the change in my mood, because the tone of his voice softens, giving me a glimpse of the Luke that I have grown to love. Luke cradles my head as he pulls me into a hug. He kisses my temple, but he gets in his truck anyway, still not extending me an invitation to come on his stress release. "I'll be back, Gi. I just..." Luke pauses. "This isn't about you, okay? I just need a minute to be alone."

Alone. Something that Luke never asks of me. To leave him alone.

"I love you, Luke." The words sound different this time. Not a confession. Not a promise. A desperate plea coming out of my mouth that he won't do anything reckless. I already lost one Palmer boy. "Promise me you'll drive safe? Don't do anything stupid?"

Luke shoots me a lopsided smile that calms my heart. "You know I always do, Gi. I wouldn't do that to you."

As he drives off with the windows down, I hear him tell me he loves me, too.

Watching Luke's truck get smaller the farther away he is, my brain starts doing its thing and overthinking. Vince's words echo over and over again like a broken radio. *It's wrong.* That's what he said. That's what Luke's father thinks of our relationship. I can't believe we got away with being together without anybody telling us what we're doing is wrong until now. Our friends just thought it was hilarious and Andrew's parents, by some miracle, didn't react as badly as I thought they would.

Luke's dad has spoken the words aloud now, and I can't unhear it.

Think of happy thoughts, Gigi. Picture the ocean. Picture the park. Picture Luke. Picture Luke. Picture Luke.

Tears sting my eyes, because the only image that's playing in my mind is Vince's disappointed face. *It's wrong.*

CHAPTER 38

Luke

When you're a prepubescent kid with a family who just got slaughtered, other children tend to make fun of you. I don't blame them. Everyone likes to gossip. I still remember what they said behind my back.

I bet Luke talks to the dead now.

I saw him creeping at the graveyard the other day.

My mama said he'll become a pyromaniac due to the trauma.

The last one might be bullshit, but it turns out, they weren't wrong. Here I am, having a goddamn food-less picnic at the graveyard where a quarter of the tombstones belong to my family, chatting with my mom as if she can talk back.

Before the fire, we weren't rich. We were barely middle class, just right above the cutoff. But we were happy. At least I was.

It fucking sucks that Dad can't see that I'm finally able to breathe again. Gigi makes me feel things that I haven't in a long time. It fucking stings when he had the audacity to lecture me on keeping up appearances for the others when he walked around a drunk slob, leaving me to clean up his mess for him like a goddamn live-in maid. It fucking punched me in the gut when he said the truth I've been sugarcoating ever since spring, though.

Stepsister. She's Andrew's girl. Or was. Or is. Or whatever happens when the other person dies before you get a chance to break up with them.

Making my way back to the front gate, I make one last stop before I drive back to Kinsdale Springs. The sun is about to rise now, shining just enough to give me a glimpse of the carved letters.

ANDREW ETHAN PALMER
January 2005 - September 2023
Now may The Lord of peace himself give you peace at all times and in every way.
2 Thessalonians 3:16

"I guess you never did listen in Sunday school, did you?" I shake my head, feeling the back of my eyes sting. "Killing yourself is a sin, you idiot." *No answer.* "What was so wrong with your life that you needed to off yourself, hm?" *No answer.* "You left me all alone." I start chuckling, like some lunatic would at four in the morning at a gravesite, proving those middle schoolers right about me. "I miss your stupid ass. Your parents, too. Gigi, too." *Gigi. Gigi. Gigi.* "I think that's why she slept with me in the first place," I say quietly. To Andrew or to myself, I'm not sure. "And I wish I was a better man to not do this and look for someone else, but I can't now. You're dead, so you don't get a say in this. You fucking left us." *Still no fucking answer.* "I'd pray for you, but I only ever came to church for the muffins, you know that." *And for you. To hang out with you.* "Wherever you are, I hope you know that I love you, but I love her, too. I'm sorry."

The sight of a woman with dark hair hovering over the kitchen counter greets me the moment I enter the house. Not Gigi, her mother. Bianca is still in her scrubs as she stirs a teaspoon of sugar into her tea.

"Your father is gone again," she says, her tone eerily calm. She's blowing her hot drink, but her eyes are on me. Watching me. Following my move from the door to the coffee machine. "He asked his colleague to switch schedules." Good, let him be gone. I don't want to see the sight of him, either. That hypocrite.

"Okay."

"You know, Luke," she sighs, "he told me about what happened and I want you to know that I don't condone it. It might not be my place to say, but Vince was grieving too. In a very problematic way, yes, but grieving nonetheless."

"You're right," I answer. The harshness of my voice matches the way I slam the coffee pot on the counter. "It's not your place to say."

"People deal with loss in different ways, Luke." In her dark eyes, I see sympathy. For Dad or for me, no clue. Bianca takes a step closer to me and sets her mug next to mine. "But enough about your dad. I won't even try to meddle. Like I said, it's not my place, Luke. I just want you to know that I can understand both sides." She lifts her hands up in the air, shooting me a small smile. "I'm not the enemy here." As I sip my black coffee with my back perched against the counter, Bianca looks at me again. "But it is my place to ask what's going on with you and Giuliana. Is this the way you two deal with your grief? By being together, you get to feel closer to Andrew?"

"I'm in love with your daughter, Bianca."

"She told me she loved you, too."

"Are you going to fight us on this?"

Would we even be on each other's radar had our parents not gotten married? Most definitely not. Gigi would probably still be in New York, living life to the fullest and infecting people with her happy smile. I would probably go through life doing the opposite, just letting life pass by me. If Andrew didn't die, would we even be here right now? The answer would also be a big fat no. The jury is out whether the two of them would still be a couple or not, but if they had broken up, Gigi would probably get snatched up by some other jock who'd probably propose to her on her graduation and whisk her away on a European summer trip as a present. And I'd be dating the likes of Autumn—girls who make me feel like I always come up short, exactly how my father makes me feel.

But for some fucked up reason, the universe decided to do its thing and change the course of our lives. Twice. God or whatever higher power out there mellowed Gigi down and gave me a chance to get to know her. Love her. Cheer her up. And for some reason I still can't quite fathom myself, Gigi doesn't make me feel like I need to be someone I'm not to make her happy. She has all the ammunition in the world to compare me to the one person I hate being compared to the most, and she hasn't used it once.

Lord knows I'm far from perfect, but when she looks at me, I feel like I could be. I feel like I want to try, so I'm going to fight for her. Even if my battle is with her own mother.

"No, Luke. I'm not," Bianca says calmly. Her chamomile tea must be working. "I'm not happy about this, but I'm going to let you both be. You've both been through a lot. I'm not going to lose my daughter because I can't accept the fact that she's dating you."

I blink. "Thank you," is all I manage to mumble.

"Besides, she could do a lot worse than you. She could've come home with a tattooed biker. Grieving people do weird things." Never have I ever come out on top in a game of who-is-the-better-pick, but I'll take this win.

"I'm not going to hurt her, Bianca," I assure Gigi's mom. "I'm serious about her."

"Oh, I know." Bianca's tired eyes soften as she smiles. "I see it all over your face. I would've told you both to break it off if it wasn't so apparent that you'd do anything for my daughter."

I chuckle, thinking that I need to get Bianca a nicer Christmas present from now on.

"Just promise me something," she says in a more serious tone.

"Shoot." This woman could ask me to lick the floor clean right now and I'd get right to it.

"I'd say no sex before marriage, but I'm not stupid, so just promise me you'll be careful? I'm not ready to be a grandmother." Fair enough. "And if you end up with Gigi, you're becoming a Catholic, Luke. Do I make myself clear?"

"Crystal."

CHAPTER 39

Gigi

I feel the sun shining through the window, alerting me that it's morning already. I turn to the side, only to feel a hard, naked chest next to me. Fluttering my eyes open, I see Luke with damp hair, smelling like soap. He has dark circles and looks like he's been up all night, but he's here. He's in one piece.

"You're back," I say, my voice raspy. My back turns, returning me to my original position, as I pull his arm and drape it over my stomach. I want to be the little spoon.

Intertwining my fingers with his, Luke pulls me closer to him. "Where else would I be?" I feel his breath on the crown of my head, caressing me as he exhales. "It's still early, Gi. Let's sleep in."

The second time I wake up, I feel his hand cupping my left breast under my shirt. The friction of his calloused skin against my nipple causes me to tilt my head back, pushing me further into his embrace. From the corner of my eye, I see a satisfied grin on Luke's face. "What time is it?" I ask, not really caring.

"Almost noon," he answers as he kisses the crook of my

neck. "Becca is with her friends and Bianca just left for a hair appointment."

I want to say something. To ask what our plan is for the day. To tell him that maybe we can visit Zach in Marble Crest. But the words die on the tip of my tongue. My brain is a jumbled mess of pleasure with both of Luke's palms now on my breasts, kneading them as his fingers play with my hardened nipples. I push my ass against his bulge, and I feel it turn rock hard behind my back. I grind against him, knowing that it will drive Luke over the edge, wanting this to go more than just touching, needing to feel a connection to him after yesterday.

"Gigi."

"I missed you yesterday." Ridiculous, really. We were apart for less than twenty-four hours. In that time span, I felt the full range of emotions, reaching the crescendo when I thought maybe he would hurt himself due to all the stress and pressure. "Where did you go, Luke?"

Luke lifts my shirt up and pulls it over my head before throwing it on the floor. He kisses me from my earlobe to my jaw as his finger trails the curve of my hip. "I was at the graveyard."

"All night?"

"Yes," he answers, grabbing my ass. "Saw your mom when I came in. She gave us her blessing."

"Really?" The question isn't supposed to come out as a breathy gasp, but when Luke inserts a finger inside my opening and slides the wetness to my clit, I feel heat radiating everywhere. "What did she say?"

"She doesn't want to be a grandmother yet," he says, smiling. With his finger still rubbing lazy circles between my thighs, he gently pushes my shoulder to the side, making me lie on my back. Honey eyes look up at me as he plants a short, teasing kiss on each of my nipples. "Told me I should become a Catholic."

I grin. I pleaded my case to her before she left for work. I'm glad it didn't go in vain. *That's Mom for you.* With how he feasts on my breasts, you'd think I have porn star tits. He sucks and licks while I run my hand through his hair with my eyes closed, enjoying the tingling sensation all over my body. He's so good at this, making me come. With his fingers. With his tongue. But right now, I want to do something else. Something that I haven't done before since Luke likes to be the one giving.

"Can I be on top today?" I ask after he gives me my first orgasm for the day.

At some point, Luke must have taken his underwear off, because his erection is staring at me. Red and veiny, ready to go. He leans his back against the headboard, giving me full access to his body. "Be my guest," he says, biting his bottom lip.

"Will you tell me what to do?" I ask as I sink myself onto him slowly. We both moan the moment his dick is fully inside of me, filling me up. Lacing my fingers at the nape of his neck to steady myself, I start moving up and down. Slowly at first, but the moment I get the hang of it, I start picking up the pace.

"You're fucking perfect, Gi," he rasps with hooded eyes. Both of his hands squeeze my ass. "Keep doing this and your mom might have to be a grandma soon."

Again, Luke's arm snakes between us, touching my still-swollen bud. As I moan, I feel myself losing my rhythm. I start to go slower, not being able to focus while having him play with me. He squeezes my right breast before both of his hands lock on my hips as he thrusts into me from below. "Touch yourself," he commands, so I continue where he left off.

We come undone together in a pool of sweat with me

moaning his name and Luke cursing. Luke doesn't push me off, instead he pulls me closer, cupping my face as he kisses me hungrily. Like he needs me to breathe.

Still panting, I stare into those honey eyes that have become a safe haven for me these past few months. My whole body heats up when I realize just how intense my feelings for him are. There is nothing I wouldn't do for this man. Luke deserves the world and I'm going to try to give it to him.

This is the real deal, Gigi. This is what it feels like to love. This is what it feels like to be loved.

CHAPTER 40

Gigi

I PUT ON MY FLOWER-SHAPED EARRINGS IN FRONT OF the mirror; the ones with the fake pearl in the middle that make me feel pretty. The golden petals complement the moss-green color of my satin dress, and the green complements the dark shade of my hair.

"Wow." My lips curve when I hear the voice. Turning around, I'm spoiled by the sight of Luke wearing beige slacks and a white, button-down dress shirt leaning on the door-frame, his suit jacket slung over his arm. "You look amazing."

I can hear the sound of my heartbeat hammering in my ears. *Dress to impress*. I spent a lot of nights searching and a lot of shifts at the restaurant to get this dress. No one has ever invited me to be their plus-one to a wedding before. If that wasn't enough pressure, Luke told me that Andrew's parents were going to come, as well. Back then, I didn't know that they'd swallow down the news of us dating semi-easily. I thought, if all else fails, at least Luke would have an arm candy as a date.

But it's him. He's the arm candy. He looks absolutely mesmerizing. The only times I've ever seen guys wear formal wear were during school dances. The man standing in front of me doesn't look like he's an acne-ridden teenager. No, Lucas Palmer is the absolute dreamboat on a stick right now.

"I'm ready!" Becca yells from her room. A few seconds later, she waltzes into my room, twirling around in her lavender-colored maxi dress that Mom picked out for her.

Luke's eyes do a double take and I swear, *I swear*, I see them turn glassy, even if it's just for a blip. Shoving one of his hands in his pocket, he stalks over to his little sister and roughs her hair up playfully, causing her to frown. "Baby sis all grown up," he says with a hint of humor. "Give me a few more years and then you're going to start dating."

"Oh, like how you and Gigi are dating?" she snaps back as she swats Luke's hand away and fixes the headband on her head.

Luke and I both stiffen and speak at the same time.

"How do you know that?"

"Who told you that?"

Becca shrugs. "Aunt Judith. She picked me up from Kimmy's house the other day."

"What do you think about me dating your brother, Becca?" I take a deep breath. It must be weird for her to know we're a couple. Becca spent years with Luke at home, and then after that she spent time bonding with me as her sister. In a way, I became a surrogate sibling. She must think we're messed up.

"I think you two look real pretty together."

I hear Luke let out a relieved breath, his eyes glittering with happiness as they steal glances at me. "Oh, yeah?" Luke asks, a grin plastered all over his face.

"Gigi makes you less grumpy, too." Now it's me who's tilting my head back, laughing. *I guess I do.*

Luke saunters away from the dance floor toward the bar, getting himself a beer and me a club soda. My eyes quickly scan for an empty chair. With the way the straps of my heels are digging into my skin, I can't stand another minute on my feet.

Click. Clack. Click. Clack. I plop myself on a wooden bank under an apple tree, thankful for the shade. My fingers directly go to the buckle of the straps before tracing the red, angry blisters. "Shit," I utter to myself. *You should've splurged on the good shoes, Gigi.*

"You're back quick!" I say when I hear footsteps approaching me, thinking Luke cut the queue of guests waiting for their drinks. When I tilt my head up, it's not him I see. It's Judith Palmer with an amused look on her face. "Sorry. I thought you were Luke."

"He's right there," she points toward the bar as she sits next to me. "So, how are you, Gigi? Enjoying the summer?"

I have a feeling she's not here to ask about my break, but I force a smile out, anyway. "Yeah, I am." I nod. "It's nice to not have to think about assignments and exams for a change. What about you, Mrs. Palmer? How are you doing?"

She ignores my question. "So I heard Vince didn't take the news of you two dating very well." Judith makes a face as she says *dating*, like it physically pains her to admit Luke and me are together out loud.

"No, he didn't. They got into a fight afterward, actually." I look over to Luke who's chatting and laughing in line with Ross, the groom. Before I can think about who I'm speaking with, my mouth decides to betray common sense. "I've never seen Luke so angry before. It was kind of scary."

"Hmm." Judith follows my line of vision and looks at her nephew, too, crossing her legs. "You know, out of everybody, Lucas is the one who had it the roughest. I was there when we heard the news about the fire." I heard about this. It was his birthday and Andrew's family took him to his game because, by some miracle, his mom and his grandma decided to call a truce during Luke's twelfth birthday and throw a party for him. *If only they never set foot in that church...*

"It must have been tough for him," I say, looking down at my lap. "He was just a kid."

"That he was. But he grew up to be an amazing young man. Broken, but amazing." Judith smiles to herself, then angles her body so that she's facing me. "Gigi, trust me that I don't mean anything malicious when I say this." She pauses, and in that span, my heart rate picks up, thumping in my chest. Nothing good ever comes after *trust me that I don't mean anything malicious when I say this.* "I don't think you and him should be in a relationship together. You two are just trauma bonding."

I fight the urge to fight her on the correct definition of trauma bonding. The phrase she's looking for is shared trauma. "That's not what we're doing," I say instead.

"Oh, honey," she coos condescendingly, making my heart cave in. *Hold it in, Gigi. This woman is important to Luke.* "I know it's confusing. You both lost Andrew and being at the same college together must be comforting. But Luke is fragile. He won't withstand a girl like you."

I flash her an angry smile. "And what kind of girl am I, Mrs. Palmer?" Andrew's dad was nothing but nice and friendly when we first got together, but his mom? She always gave me fake niceties, being sweet when her son was around and cold the moment he left the room. I always knew that she thought Andrew deserved better than me, the big city girl whose working mother married a tourist bus driver.

Her lips thin as she lets out a breath through her nose. "You know, my son left to go to your house one night and came home drunk out of his mind with a busted lip. What happened, Gigi? He didn't tell me what happened, but I was also young once. I know what pretty girls are like." *Which night is she talking about?* "Making the boys fight over them."

"I never asked him to do that!" I defend myself, still clueless as to which night she's fucking referring to. Something like that did happen, but it was only once. He wasn't drunk and he ended up sleeping in my room, only leaving the day after. Andrew didn't fight. It wasn't his thing. He was the binge-drink-but-nothing-else kind of guy.

"You might not have asked him, but he did it anyway, dear." Judith raises her tone as her jaw clenches. "He started dating you and the next thing we know, he turned into a mess, getting into fights, partying, and..." Her eyes are filled with angry tears and they're all directed at me. "Killed himself." My unshed ones are dropping now, streaming down my perfectly made-up face. *Did I do that to Andrew?* "Imagine what Luke would be like. Please, Giuliana. Be a smart girl. Think this through. You might not mean it, but Luke will end up hurt. He's even more vulnerable than Andrew."

"Think through what?" Judith goes rigid next to me, her head tilting upward to face her nephew while mine stay planted on the ground, only giving me a glimpse of his leather Oxford shoes.

"Luke! I didn't see you come." Again, she goes with the fake smile and the giggle. "I was just asking Gigi how her summer was."

Luke regards his aunt for a second before his jaw clenches. "I don't think that's what I heard, Aunt Judith."

"Look," she answers as she puts a hand on the side of her head, resting her elbow on her lap. "I think you two are making a mistake."

"I'm not making a mistake."

"Honey, you're young and grieving. I know it feels good to have someone, but do you really think Gigi—"

"Don't talk about Gigi like she's not there, Aunt Judith,"

Luke cuts her off. "If you can't get on board with this, then I'm sorry. But I'm not going to change my mind."

Andrew's mom stands up, her heels digging into the ground. "Very well then," she sighs as she smooths out her dress. "Have a nice summer break."

CHAPTER 41
Gigi

SEVENTEEN YEARS OLD

THE CROWD ROARS. ONE HALF IS JUMPING UP AND down in joy while the other is chanting for a rematch. The football team of Kinsdale Springs High just beat its opponent —the guys from Marble Crest.

My eyes glint with pride as they search for my boyfriend in a sea of people. Andrew told me he'd come today. When he does make it to these games, he usually sits on our side of the stadium. He's here to watch me cheer, after all. The guy doesn't even care about football and he doesn't try to hide it. Since today's match is against his own school, I squint my eyes to try and find him on the other side of the field. Maybe he's there.

"Have you seen Andrew?" I ask Lauren, my best friend.

"Sorry, babe." She shakes her head.

"Maybe he sat on the other side," Lauren's boyfriend, Bryan, chimes in as he drapes his arm around her shoulders. "It's his school, after all."

"Nope." Not there, either. "Maybe he's waiting for me in the parking lot."

"Tell him his school's football team sucks, Gigi," Bryan jokes with a smug grin.

"You stink, Bryan," I say with a smirk. "Go shower."

Turning on my heel, I take my phone out and open the messaging app.

Where are you?

Twenty minutes pass by and Andrew still hasn't responded to me. My fingers start tapping on my screen as I wait for him to answer. I was sure that he would've shown up outside the changing room, but here I am, all changed and still no sign of my boyfriend.

Should I catch a ride with someone else?

One by one, cars start exiting the parking lot, leaving in droves to go to the after-party. I sit cross-legged on the sidewalk, waiting for the owner of the blue SUV, one of the only vehicles still parked here, to come out.

Did you get diarrhea or something?

Just as I am about to call Lauren and ask her whether it's too late for Bryan to turn around and for them to give me a lift, I see two jean-clad legs walk toward me. "I got caught up. Sorry."

I take the hand he's offering and lift myself up. I'm about to give him the cold shoulder for not replying to my texts and making me sit out here in the cold when my eyes widen at the sight of his bloody knuckles. "Andrew, what the fuck?"

Andrew's eyes meet mine and they're filled with an expression I can't make out. His dirty blond hair is disheveled. The skin on his right cheekbone is red, which I'm sure will turn into a bruise. I look at him up and down to make sure his battle scars aren't accompanied by a stab wound somewhere.

"Got into a fight." *No shit, Sherlock.*

"With whom?" I ask, almost thinking he's joking. I might have only known him since November last year, but Andrew doesn't get into fights. He's the guy who makes a fool of himself at parties because he thinks it's funny. He's everyone's friend. Literally, every single person that I have introduced him to gushed about how much they like him.

"It doesn't matter, babe." He's giving me a look to please just drop this conversation. *Nuh uh.* "Can we skip the party at Mackenzie's today? I'm not in the mood."

"Only if you tell me what happened," I say, using this as my way in.

"Gigi, just drop it." Andrew takes my hand and starts leading me to his car, gripping it tight.

"Tell me what happened, please," I plead, halting my steps. "Tell me and then we can go home to my place. Mom's working and Becca is at a sleepover." I take his wounded hand and hold it with both of mine, tracing my finger on the red, swollen knuckles before stopping when he hisses. "Let's clean you up."

"Fine," he finally relents. "An idiot from my school was making comments about you. Said you looked really hot in your cheer outfit."

"You don't beat a guy up for saying that, Andrew."

"That's not why I punched him," Andrew sighs. He pulls me closer to him, resting his hands on the curve of my back. "I did it because he said he'd like to fuck you and make me watch."

Small town boys are idiots. This is what happens when you have nothing else better to do. You rile each other up. I guess it must get boring for the kids at Marble Crest High, too.

CHAPTER 42
Luke

TWO WEEKS LATER

I COME UP WITH A LOT OF SHITTY IDEAS. TRULY. Ridiculous ones. Going back home to Kinsdale Springs with Gigi was definitely one of them.

Being in love blinds you to a lot of things. It turns you fucking delusional. I know I did because there I was, thinking that everything would turn out fine and everyone would welcome us with open arms. Yet here I am, about to be dumped by my girlfriend.

"Gi, fucking sit down for a minute, will you?" I grab her wrist with the hope that she'll stop packing the two suitcases that she brought all the way from Ravensfield.

"My flight is tomorrow, Luke. I need to get everything ready and you should go to church," she answers coldly.

Ah, yes. Church. The reason Gigi went from zero to one hundred in a matter of hours. Not that our relationship wasn't already steadily going down since Aunt Judith scared her off. I have watched in real time how my girlfriend turned from warm and loving into an ice cube. Fun summer.

"I told you; I'm not fucking going there," I try to temper my voice as I shove both hands in my pockets. "Not until this whole thing blows over."

"And I told you, you should go," she says, her voice raised. "Seriously, you're making it worse. They already think I corrupted Andrew. I don't need to be blamed for this, too. Besides, you're Becca's ride."

"Becca will survive missing one Sunday." *She'll hate me for it, though. She really likes Sunday school.*

Turning around, Gigi gives me a sarcastic laugh. My heart caves when I see sadness in the gray of her eyes. I thought she was kidding when she said Aunt Judith doesn't like her. I put her in this position. We should've eased the family into it instead of me shouting from the rooftop that she's mine. *Fuck.*

"Luke," she drawls my name out bitterly. "I will not be responsible for a whole generation of Palmers skipping church. Just fucking go."

"Will you *not* go to New York tomorrow if I go?" I'd follow her if I could, but I can't afford the last-minute plane ticket.

The moment I told her last night that I wasn't going to go to Marble Crest today because I'm still pissed off at my aunt, she had a mental breakdown. Gigi started rambling about how my family already thinks that she was a bad influence on Andrew. The nonsense continued with her pleading with me to go to church tomorrow because she didn't want to be accused of the same thing with me. After I said no again and we had our first official fight, she took her dad up on his offer and booked a plane ticket so that she could spend the rest of her summer with him.

"I'm going to get on that flight, Luke." Her voice is breaking, making her sound younger than she actually is. Less confident. I've never seen this side of her before. I guess that's what happens when the mother of your dead ex-boyfriend indirectly blames you for his suicide.

"Gi, please," I say, scrubbing a hand over my face. "Leaving over something like this is a bit melodramatic, don't you think?"

I can already feel her slipping away from me. In a big city like that, surrounded by her old friends and millions of people. Would someone else comfort her during a night out when she's had one too many and decides to spill her heart out? Is someone going to tell her to dump me, the small town nobody?

She has always been out of my league, even without the complications. Is she finally going to realize that once she's there? Leave me for the guy who's going to gift her a giant rock during her graduation and whisk her away to her happily ever after?

"You need to spend more time with your family," she answers coldly. "And I want to see my dad. Maybe some space will do us good."

"Some space," I scoff. "That's just your way of being too chickenshit to break up with me. If this is too hard for you, Gi, just say so. Don't talk in circles like you've been doing for the past two weeks."

The flash of hurt on her face makes my back go rigid. That and realizing what I just said. I always do this. Self-sabotage when I feel the girl is losing interest in me. Become the dumper before you become the dumpee. *This is not some girl you slept with in high school, Luke. This is not Autumn. Shut the fuck up.*

"Gi, I didn't mean it like that." She says nothing, going back to putting small bottles inside a Ziploc bag. "Talk to me," I say softly, grabbing her forearm. "Gi, I'm sorry."

"Maybe we should." I feel like someone just crushed my

heart. "I don't think I'm a good influence on you. I clearly wasn't one to Andrew."

I stare at her, not knowing what to say. At my girlfriend who's breaking up with me, comparing me to my cousin and using that as an argument. Hurt doesn't even begin to express what I'm feeling inside.

"Luke! We're going to be late!" Becca screams from downstairs. "Are we going or not?"

"Just go, Luke." *What the actual fuck?* How did my life go from cuddling with her in her dorm to this? But instead of me who's not giving her the time of day, it's the other way around. This must be my karma.

"Are you going to be here when I get back?" I ask, my feet planted on the carpet.

"Sure."

At church, Aunt Judith tries to justify what she said to Gigi, not backing down even for a bit. I start to wonder whether she really sees my girlfriend as someone who's responsible for Andrew's downfall, or she just needed a scapegoat. Andrew made his own choices in life. Whatever his reason was, the fucker took it with him. Does she really need to blame Gigi because her son didn't have the decency to share his reason?

Coming back home, I find her room empty and her suitcase gone. There is a note on the bed addressed to me.

Changed my flight to an earlier one. By the time you read this my phone will probably be off. I'll text you once I land. We need space, Luke. Fighting sucks.
Love, Gigi

If I wasn't so mad at Aunt Judith, I would tell her what I know now. Getting a goodbye letter stings as much as not getting one.

CHAPTER 43
Gigi

START OF THE NEW SEMESTER, A MONTH LATER.

"LUKE, PLEASE OPEN UP!" I YELL, BANGING ON THE door. "Please. I know I messed up. I'm here now."

Music is blaring from inside his apartment. There is no way he's not inside. Either he's in there or Kai is in there. I turn on my heel, about to make my way down the hallway, thinking they probably can't hear me, but then my mind decides to remind me of how Luke found Andrew.

Think of happy thoughts, Gigi. Picture the ocean. Picture the park. Picture...picture Luke holding you in his arms.

"Luke!" I knock again, my voice this time frantic. "Luke, please! It's me. It's G—"

I'm both relieved and disappointed to see Kai open the door. Judging by the frown he's wearing, he's not all that happy to find me standing on the other side as well.

"Gigi," he sighs out my name. "What's up?"

"Is Luke in there?" I peer behind him, trying to find a mop of dirty blond locks in a small crowd of guys laughing and shoving pizza slices down their throats. "I need to speak to him. He's not picking up my calls."

"Yeah. He's here." Curt. Cold. Luke must have told him.

God, I fucked up. Flying to Dad. Telling Luke we need space. *Shit.* By the end of my trip, uneasiness started to come and go inside me and guilt racked up. Big time. But Luke wasn't having it. My last week there, I texted him multiple times to say we should talk. His answer?

You want space. You got it.

The few weeks I spent in New York made me realize how I messed things up. On my flight and train ride back to Ravensfield, it was crystal clear to me how much of an idiot I was. I guess Luke came to the same conclusion.

"I need to talk to him, Kai."

Kai presses his lips together. My puppy eyes are not working on him. "Give it some time, Gigi. He's really upset with you." *Shit.* "Like really upset," Kai emphasizes.

"I know," I whisper. "That's why I'm here. I want to apologize."

Luke's best friend hesitates for a second, making sounds as if he's debating letting me in. "Wait here a sec."

Still in the doorway, I feel my phone vibrate in my pocket. My eyebrows scrunch when I see who's calling. *Michael Palmer.* He never calls me.

"Hello," I answer, cupping my other ear to make sure I can hear him with all this music.

"Gigi, how are you?"

"I'm fine." *Your wife blames me for your son's death, but it's cool.* "Is something wrong? Did something happen with Vince or Becca?"

"No. No, dear. I was hoping we could talk." My heart thuds in my chest. I feel it. Another confrontation is coming. He's going to tell me how fucked up it is for me to date Luke. He's about to rescind his blessing.

"Uh, okay."

"With both you and Luke, actually. But Luke is not picking up my calls. He hasn't been since...you know, what happened at the wedding." His tone is somber. I appreciate that it's not accusatory.

I'm tempted to tell Andrew's dad that he might have a better chance of actually reaching Luke than me, but then I see Kai back at the door. "Can I call you back? I'm sorry. I'm in the middle of something."

"Of course. Feel free to reach out to me whenever you're available. Have a nice night, Giuliana."

"So..." I look up at Kai feeling somewhat hopeful, putting my phone away. "What's the verdict?"

He lifts his hands up in the air, blowing air out of his mouth. Kai's smile is telling me he's sorry. "I tried."

I feel like I'm running out of air. This is it. He's going to dump me. I let Judith's words become a self-fulfilling prophecy.

You might not mean it, but Luke will end up hurt.

"Thanks, Kai," I manage to say.

"I'll try talking to him again. He can't keep this up forever. Take it easy, Gigi."

"Yeah. You too."

I bolt out of their building as fast as I could. I don't want Kai to see my tears. I don't even deserve to cry. This is all my doing. Luke was ready to risk it all and what did I do? I cowered.

Outside his building, I shoot Luke a text, pouring my heart out and hoping he'll understand.

> You already got a million of these, but I'm going to send another one. I love you, Luke. I'm sorry.

LUKE

This might have worked a few days after you left. Hell, the week after that, even. But you went to your dad's and gave me the bare minimum for a month, Gi. Do you seriously expect me to not be upset right now?

Well, I'm here now and I want to fix it. I know I did wrong. I really need to talk to you.

Have a taste of your own medicine.

CHAPTER 44

Luke

I THROW MY PHONE ON THE MATTRESS, MY ANGER reaching its limit. Fuck Gigi, fuck Aunt Judith, and Fuck Kai for hosting this hangout without asking me first.

"Dude," one source of my fury says. I can't see him with my back facing the door, but I know Kai is there. "Don't make me shoo away a fucking crying girl from the door again. You're a dick for this."

"She was crying?" I ask, turning around.

"Might as well be. For what it's worth, I think she's really sorry."

I figured. And God damn it, a part of me knows that she really is. Aunt Judith was brutal. But that doesn't excuse the fact that she just left. She flew to her dad's. Aunt Judith spooked her and she pulled away from me. We were saying *I love yous* to each other like we were supposed to last forever. I guess I was the only one who thought so.

Gigi didn't break up with me in New York, but she didn't put in much effort, either. If I have to read another text saying *I need space*, I think I might explode.

Rejection is never a good thing. Laying yourself bare for

the first time and then have the other person walking away, fucking running, at the first sign of trouble? Can a relationship really last like that?

Kai claps me on the back before going back outside to our friends. "Don't be so fucking stubborn, Luke."

I groan when I see the sight of my girlfriend running toward me. Her dark hair flies all over her face as she repeatedly calls out to me, clutching her laptop in her hand.

"Not now, Gi," I finally answer, trying not to cause a scene. "I have class."

"Skip it. It's syllabus week." Her doe eyes are filled with something I can't make out. Desperation? Hope? Heartbreak? Maybe the three swirled into one, forming two gray circles that look like a shiny stone. "I have something important to tell you."

"Gigi." Her name comes out with a sigh. "We can talk about it tonight or tomorrow. I'll call you. Just not now. I really have to go."

"Skip your class, Luke. You're going to want to hear this. There are a few things that we need to discuss."

"No," I scoff. "I'm on scholarship. I'm about to lose it." *Because it's contingent on me performing well, and I haven't been doing as good since Andrew died.* "I'm not going to skip shit. And while I'm there, I suggest you also go to yours. Stop begging your boyfriend to spend time with you like a petulant fucking child."

We both snap our eyes to each other the moment I mention the word boyfriend. Yeah, I've decided that I'm still her boyfriend. She's still mine. I'm just so goddamn pissed at her still. I'm saving my energy for that inevitable talk that we're going to have to have. My aunt is my problem to handle, but Gigi is going to get an earful from me about what she did.

"I'm...I'm not..." she stutters. "I'm not a petulant child."

"Then stop acting like one," I grit out.

"You need to pick up your uncle's calls." My eyebrows shoot up. This is not what I was expecting her to say.

"You're cornering me in the library because you want me to take Uncle Mike's calls?"

"Yes," she says. "Among other things. But this is the most pressing one right now."

"Why?"

"Because Andrew made a video before he died, and your uncle showed it to me last night."

I need air. I need to breathe. I need...I don't know what I need.

My vision blurs as I try to remember what happened before I turned my phone on silent and went to sleep. Kai left my room and a few hours later, Uncle Mike called me about ten times, all of them dodged just like the ones before. Gigi must have tried about twice as much, all of them sent to voicemail as well. I didn't want to talk to either of them.

I open my messaging app in front of her, cursing myself when I read through the one-sided chain of texts.

GIGI

Have fun at your party. I'm sorry if I embarrassed you in front of your friends.

Luke, your uncle is telling us to come to Marble Crest. He said it's important.

I swear it's not a ploy to get you to forgive me. But we do need to talk.

Can you please pick up?

I don't have a car. I can't go to Marble Crest alone. The bus is not running anymore.

Your uncle said he's going to pay for my Uber. It must be really important.

My driver will be here soon if you want to join.

Then I finally read the last one.

We need to talk about Andrew.

CHAPTER 45

Gigi

THE NIGHT BEFORE

I LAUGH WHEN I SEE ANDREW'S DAD PLUGGING IN the USB stick. *This is so Andrew.* He likes analog cameras and record players. He prefers going to the movies over streaming. Of course he wouldn't upload his goodbye to a cloud or send it as an attachment via email.

The moment the video starts playing, I feel my cheeks getting warm and wet. Sitting in his dining room feels much like being in a time machine. It's been a while since I've heard that voice. Since I've seen that face. His dad gives me a sad, knowing look when I stop myself from tracing the curve of his jaw on the screen.

"So, uh, hey guys," Andrew said to his camera. *When did he record this? That's his dorm room. I put that poster up on his wall.* "If you're watching this, that means I'm dead."

Sucking in a breath, I look at the ceiling. *Oh, God.*

Think of happy thoughts, Gigi. Picture the—

My name gets called out and I snap back to reality. A lopsided smile. Loving blue eyes. I feel like I'm about to vomit.

"Gigi, Gigi, Gigi." He whistled and I laugh. "The firecracker who stole Luke's bedroom. I had such a huge crush on you when we met. Felt like the luckiest guy alive, too, when I finally wore you down after months and made you go out with me." Andrew paused to crack his knuckles before his eyes returned back to the camera. "You know I don't deserve you, right? I'm sorry and I wish I would have met you earlier. You would have gotten the better version of me for some time longer. Promise me you won't be sad for too long, babe?" *He fucking grinned.* "We both know your forever man was always going to be someone better than me. Don't let me stop you. Just get a tattoo of me or something to remember me by."

My sob gets louder when I hear his last words for me.

"Thanks for allowing me to fall in love with you."

I loved you, Andrew Ethan Palmer. I'm sorry for not saying it. A part of me will always love you. You were my first boyfriend. My first kiss. And a lot of other firsts. Take care, wherever you are.

"Thank you for showing this," I say to his dad the moment he pauses the video. "I'm really sorry for everything with Luke, Mr. Palmer." He must be crushed right now. His son declared his love for me on screen while I was here two months ago as his nephew's girlfriend. "I understand if you would want me to keep my distance from him."

Andrew's dad stares at his laptop and then at me, pensive. Twin lines appear on his forehead as he lets out a long breath. "Watch the video until the end, Gigi."

"Oh? Is he going to address me again?"

"No."

I frown at his words. "Then it's okay. Seeing this is already more than enough. I don't need to hear what he said to anyone else. It's like eavesdropping."

It feels wrong to listen to someone's last words that aren't meant for you. Like a broken promise or snooping through other people's things. *Maybe I can ask Andrew's dad whether he can cut the video and send me a copy of the part he just played.*

"I want you to," Andrew's dad says. "I think you should."

"Alright." And then he presses play.

"Luuuuke." I feel goosebumps stand on the nape of my neck. "I've been a shit friend, haven't I? I just wanted to let you try out life. Be you for once, you know? Plus, I'd much rather spend my time with my girlfriend than you. If Gigi deserves better than me, you deserve better than Kinsdale Springs. And boy, was I right. You're cooler as a college dude than a high school kid. Go be a stockbroker or whatever. I'll haunt you if you end up as a loser. But remember, don't forget to have fun. Stop being so serious all the time, man." The moment Andrew gives Luke a goodbye wink, I take out my phone and text him, my heart thundering inside my ribcage.

We need to talk about Andrew.

I'm about to text Luke more when the sound of Andrew's voice halts me. My fingers turn rigid the moment I hear the six-word sentence. "Mom, Dad is cheating on you."

I look up, horrified, to see Mr. Palmer staring straight at me. My throat is dry. *Should I say something?*

"Just watch, Gigi," he says, gesturing to the laptop.

Unlike the message for me and Luke, Andrew wasn't smiling anymore by the time he got to this part. This Andrew, this one is the one I remember from our last year of high school.

"He's been cheating on you with a lot of other women." *What the fuck?* "He slept with a high school student, too. Isn't that right, Dad? You want to tell Mom about Rachel?" *What the actual fuck?* "I caught him one night with a woman and he made me keep it a secret. He swore up and down it was a one-time thing. Some pillar of the community he is." Next to me, Andrew's dad is gripping the edge of the dining table so hard his knuckles are starting to turn white. It's like watching a fucking trainwreck; my eyes are glued to Andrew's scowl, waiting for him to say more. "Get a goddamn divorce, Mom. Before his secrets ruin you, too...I'm sorry. I'm so sorry and I love you. Please forgive me for this."

My hands are trembling. I don't think I can watch this any longer. I just know it. I'm so close. We're at the finish line. The video is about three-quarters done, and by the time the red line catches up to the white one...I will know everything. The answer to the question I've been asking myself over and over again for close to a year.

The sneer from Andrew makes it clear that he saved the best for last—a final message for his father. Michael Palmer. The pastor. The doting dad. The cheater. *The man who had sex with a high school girl my age.* I'm going to be sick.

"You know that parents are supposed to clean up their children's messes, right, Dad? Not the other way around? You told me it was a drunken mistake. Well, his mom didn't think so." *Whose Mom?* "And he made sure I paid for it. For your fucking sins." I hold my hand over my mouth, already feeling the bile rise up to my throat. *What the hell is Andrew talking about?* "He made my life a living hell, did you know that? By the end of senior year, I didn't even know who I was anymore. Want to know the worst part? I ended up being just like you. He tricked me into thinking he was into Rachel." *Oh my God.* "I just wanted to hurt him back." *Holy shit.* "And after I was done fucking her, he laughed and told me that you fucked her, too, the week before at the church's parking lot. And the worst part of it is, it didn't take me much to take the bait. I guess I am your son, after all."

"Mr. Palmer..."

He says nothing, his eyes still glued to the screen. Mine can only make out the outline of Andrew with all the tears blurring my vision.

"I went to college thinking it would be a fresh start for me. But he's here, Dad. You made his mom think you were getting a divorce, didn't you? And dumped her after she told his dad that she was leaving? Lucky me. He already promised to make me pay for what you did here, too. I'm done with his mind games. He's trying to ruin my life. Joke's on him, because I won't be here for him to do it the second time. And I won't stick around to watch you fuck all of our lives up as well. I saw you, Dad. You don't have a shred of dignity, do you? I saw your car on campus yesterday parked in front of the theology department. Who the fuck is she? A faculty member? A student? I fucking go to school here. Why can't you have the decency to find a random girl to fuck somewhere else? That's three so far. How many are there?"

I have no idea what Andrew says after that because by the time it clicks in my brain why Andrew was in such a bad mood the night we took a stroll checking out the university layout, the first time we passed by the theology building, I'm already throwing up on the Palmers' dining room floor.

CHAPTER 46
Luke

ANDREW IS STILL DEAD.

Uncle Mike is a serial cheater.

Rachel slept with both my uncle and my cousin.

My fists are both clenched tight to my sides. If the man standing in front of me hadn't practically raised me, if I thought he wasn't already punished enough by his son being six feet underground, I'd fucking kill him.

"How long have you had this for?" I ask, seething.

"When they gave me his things," my uncle admits. Deep inside, I know. I remember seeing the stick still plugged into Andrew's laptop when I found him. But I was praying that he was going to tell me he just found it.

"Why now?"

"I didn't think it was right." I can't help but scoff. *Didn't think it was right.* He grabs the back of the chair across from me, pausing. "Judith blamed Giuliana for Andrew acting out. For him...killing himself. You stopped coming here. I didn't want her to lose you too."

"So you didn't care that we all went on for so long

thinking he didn't say goodbye?" I snap. I glare at Uncle Mike who's not saying anything.

At least he has the decency to look guilty. Aunt Judith is standing right next to him. I already know that she's going to stay with him. They will sweep this under the rug and continue on with their lives as if none of this ever came to light. I thought my family couldn't get more messed up. People surprise you every day.

"Get an STD test, Aunt Judith." I rise from my seat. "And Uncle Mike, don't bother calling me after this. I won't pick up."

My eyes burn the whole way back to Ravensfield. Driving in my truck, only one thought looms in my mind.

Andrew was angry when he said his last words to his dad. He was sorry when he bid farewell to his mom. He was trying to be cheerful for me. But the way those blue eyes lit up on screen when he addressed Gigi... At the end of his fucked up life, he died in love with Gigi.

I wonder how she feels now. About us. About him. About me.

I guess there's only one way to find out.

"I'm in front of your building," I say to her on the phone.

I hear the sound of her bed creaking followed by footsteps, telling me she's about to let me in. "See you in a sec."

I feel tingles everywhere, especially on my face, as cold sweat drips down my forehead. I know for a fact that I'm in love with her. Probably as much as Andrew was, maybe even more, but you don't come back from seeing your ex-boyfriend smile and swoon at you like that without feeling some type of way. She didn't walk out of Andrew's childhood home unscathed yesterday.

I want to punch myself for not making up with her sooner. Why did I act all cold toward her when she was ready to talk and make up? For the sake of it? Out of pettiness? Because I was a bitter asshole and had to one-up her? To push her away, not wanting to get hurt? I should have known. My days with her are probably numbered now. I should have put a dent in my savings and bought a ticket to New York to go after her.

"You saw the video," she says, crossing her hand over her stomach. I didn't pay much attention to how she looked yesterday at the library, and I wish I did. Dark circles are under her eyes and she's not wearing makeup. Gigi is the type of girl who doesn't leave the house without putting at least three products on her face. Her hair is in a messy ponytail and fuck me...she's wearing a Marble Crest High sweater. A pit grows in my stomach seeing her in his outfit. *She misses him.*

I want to ask her where her head is at. I want to ask her what this means for us. But I don't. Gigi doesn't need me to pester her about the status of our relationship right now and I'm too chickenshit to do it, anyway.

I nod. "I saw the video."

"You know about your uncle."

"I know about my uncle."

"About Rachel, too."

"Yep."

"Who do you think he was talking about?" Gigi asks. "The son of the woman your uncle was cheating with?" Her arms wrap around my waist as she sobs on my shirt. It feels less natural to hug her now; it feels wrong somehow. Like I'm hugging someone else's girlfriend. *She's wearing his sweater.* "God, it's all so fucked up, Luke," she cries.

"I know, Gi." I rub her hair from the root to the tip, and then do it repeatedly. "I'm sorry I ignored you yesterday. We should've done it together."

"He seemed so sad." Gigi looks up at me with tears streaming all over her cheeks. My thumb catches some of it as I caress her face. "I was a horrible girlfriend, Luke. He was bullied, and depressed, and sad, and I didn't even realize it. I was just so mad about Rachel."

I was a terrible cousin, too. A terrible friend. If I had to bet on it, I'd say he didn't show up to church because he couldn't stand the hypocrisy of listening to his father preaching about love and doing good, but instead of asking him properly about it, I just got butt-hurt and took his word when he said he wanted to spend more time with Gigi. I should've been there for him. I should've fucking helped him.

We failed him. Every single one of us did nothing. We were all so wrapped up in ourselves that we missed the signs that this other person was suffering, wilting away...wanting out of the life he had.

"Promise me you'll tell me?" She bites her bottom lip as she hugs me even tighter. "I know you've had a lot of things happen to you, Luke. Promise me, if you ever feel like things get too heavy for you that you'll talk to me? Don't shut me out and don't keep it to yourself."

Feeling the burn in the back of my eyes, I suck in a breath. "If you promise me you won't shut me out, too. It hurt, Gi," I say honestly. "When you went to New York. When you dodged my calls. When you asked for space to think." I kiss her forehead and my mind wanders to the portion of our summer vacation where I went from sad, to disappointed, to angry. I have so much of those three emotions sitting inside of me, I don't want to drive them all toward Gigi. Not even to Aunt Judith or my uncle. I'm just sick of feeling so down all the time. I'm going to be the next Andrew if I don't reign it in. "I've never been scared of losing a girl before. I felt like I was losing you." *I feel like I'm going to lose you now.*

"I just needed time to process everything, Luke. The

things your aunt said knocked the wind out of me. It made me think long and hard about how my life has been and who I was as a girlfriend to Andrew. Who I am as a girlfriend to you."

Is this the part where she dumps me?

"We don't have to talk about this right now," I say, trying to prolong the shelf life of my relationship with her.

Taking my hand, she gives me a sad smile that cracks my heart a bit. "Come on, let's go inside. We can talk about Andrew some more. People are starting to stare."

CHAPTER 47
Gigi

I TAKE OFF MY FLIP-FLOPS AND DIRECTLY PLOP myself on the bed. It's been a tiring two days. Horrible? I'm not sure. Cathartic? Maybe. But I also have questions now. New ones that never crossed my mind before.

Luke closes the door to my dorm room, but instead of joining me like he usually did before summer break, he just stands there, biting the inside of his cheek. His eyes narrow on me and a frown appears on his face.

"Luke, what's wrong?"

"Do you miss him?" he asks, sounding unsure. "I'm an asshole, Gi. But I need to know. Seeing that video...does that change how you feel about me?"

I feel a pull in my stomach. Two Palmer boys. Both fighting two completely different beasts in their minds. Both tortured in their own ways. Both broken yet beautiful, worthy of love and worthy of peace.

"Yes, I miss him." I flash him a sad smile when I see him nod with a look in his eyes like he's just about ready to accept defeat. But Luke was the one who told me it was okay to think of Andrew; I'm not about to lie to him. "And no, it doesn't change how I feel about you. I love you, Luke. I miss Andrew, but I love you."

"He loved you, too. I saw it all over his face. He loved you so goddamn much."

"Did seeing the video change how you feel about me?"

Luke shakes his head. Closing the distance between us, he takes a few steps and sits on the edge of my bed. "But I feel guilty now about my feelings for you," he says, looking at the floor. "Like in the beginning. After we first had sex. I felt so fucking guilty, Gi. I felt like I stole his girlfriend."

I think the biggest tragedy in life is not being able to talk to the dead. So many words left unsaid. So many questions that won't get answers. So many apologies that you just can't make. But we can't ask Andrew for permission or forgiveness now. No matter how much I want to be able to hear his voice again.

"Remember what you told me once?" I can hear my own voice breaking as I fight back my tears. "You told me he'd want us to be happy."

"Yeah."

"Do you think that he's happy for us? Because I think he is."

Luke lies down next to me and pulls me to his chest. I hear his heartbeat, fast in the beginning and then slowing down as he breathes out. When I lift my chin to look up at him, he gives me a small kiss on the crown of my head, his gaze never leaving the wall. "It's going to be the anniversary of his death soon. Want to go to his grave?"

"I do."

Still with a somber look on his face, Luke caresses my hair as he asks me a question that makes me feel queasy. "Do you think we're a good couple? What if we rocked the boat and destroyed his family all for nothing? I'm pretty sure Uncle Mike would've hidden that video like a dirty secret if Aunt Judith hadn't gone apeshit on you."

I feel the lump suddenly lodged in my throat at the mention of his aunt and uncle. I don't know how I feel about Andrew's mom, but his dad? He's a special kind of deadbeat. A different brand than Vince, but a deadbeat, nonetheless. Good thing he believes in heaven and hell, because he's getting a one-way ticket to the latter.

"I think we need some work," I tell Luke honestly. "Anything bigger than this, I don't know, Luke." I fidget in his arms.

"We're at maximum capacity, Gi." Luke's gaze bores into mine as he flashes me a defeated smile. "On the bright side, I don't think there's anything worse than this. It can only go up from here."

I nod but swallow the bile rising in my throat.

Just when I think Luke is about to fall asleep, he barks out a bitter laugh. "My uncle is insane, for God's sake. If I were you, I'd honestly dump me. My family is a fucking mess. Uncle Mike is a fucking creep. The person who's supposed to be the beacon of hope."

"Your family is my family, too, Luke." Legally speaking, it's true. There's no point in denying it.

"Don't remind me." He groans next to me, but at least he cracks a smile at my joke. "Makes me feel like a creep."

"Sorry to break it to you, buddy. But you're banging your stepsister. We are kind of creepy."

My heart warms when I hear him chuckle. I haven't heard that in a while. There were many nights I spent in New York when all I wanted to do was hear him laugh. But I didn't contact him for a reason. A stupid fucking reason, but something that I can't bring up right now. Not after that video.

We're at maximum capacity

You need to tell him, Gigi.

"Luke," I say his name slowly, my tone so soft I don't

know if he can hear me. "Do you remember? Before all this, I really wanted to talk to you."

"Don't run away from me anymore, Gi. Don't pull that shit again. Ever," he murmurs into my hair.

"I'm sorry. I was going to call you once I got there, but...I couldn't. Something happened and I needed some time to think. For myself."

"Well what a crock of shit that was. Aunt Judith got you worked up for nothing."

"Yeah, that." I manage to smile. The month was so long, by the end of it I forgot why I even left for New York in the first place. "That's not the reason why I didn't...couldn't really talk to you, Luke."

Luke jerks up, pushing himself to a sitting position. I follow suit as my heart hammers.

We're at maximum capacity.

You need to tell him, Gigi.

"Gi, did something happen while you were in New York?" His eyes are accusing me of something. If he only knew how I spent the month of August, he'd laugh at his own reaction.

Think of happy thoughts, Gigi. Picture the ocean. Picture the park. Picture how your babcia held your hair and lectured you on what to do.

"It's not what you think." I shake my head.

"Just tell me, then," Luke groans. "It's been a long day. Please."

We're at maximum capacity.

You need to tell him, Gigi.

"Luke, I needed some time for myself because I needed it to process."

"Process what?" His tone is still patient, but the way he's scratching his head tells me Luke is getting impatient with me.

Just spit it out, Gigi.

"I'm pregnant."

When I landed in New York and felt like I had the mother of all stomach bugs, migraines included, I spent a week glued to my bed. It was worse than spring break. I wasn't kidding when I told Luke that I was sick and needed the rest.

The week after, when I realized I stupidly never rescheduled my appointment for the Depo-Provera shot, I was too busy Googling how long it takes before the effects wear off. Stupid, but true. So incredibly moronic. I decided to choose this exact method because I didn't want to be like my mother. Condoms break and pills need to be taken religiously. With this, silly me thought I'd only need to go to the clinic every few months and that's it. It was the perfect solution for my forgetful self. My smartass didn't consider the fact that I'd actually forget to put in the reminder on my new phone.

By the third week, I had an inkling that something was wrong with me. When my grandmother told me to visit her without my dad one day and ordered me to pee on a stick after seeing me retching up every single one of my favorite dishes she cooked for me, I was almost certain of my fate. I swore her to secrecy and allowed myself a few days of panic where I paced around New York like a panicked madwoman.

During my final week in the city I grew up in, I was busy crafting apology after apology to Luke and figuring out how to tell him all of this. I'd imagine his reaction, have a mental breakdown, play a different scenario in my head, only to have another mental breakdown. But at this point, I'd avoided deep conversations with him long enough, he'd given up trying to reach out. It would've been the most outrageous thing to just drop the bomb on him like that when I was miles away.

Seeing Luke's reaction, I fight back the urge to cry. Luke stares at me blankly and says one word. One single word. "Fuck."

We're way past the maximum capacity.

CHAPTER 48

Andrew

START OF FRESHMAN YEAR

DARRYL, MY NEW ROOMMATE, CLOSES THE DOOR TO the room that will be my home for the foreseeable future. How long that is, is still up for debate.

The moment I can't hear his footsteps anymore, I grab my book from the nightstand. *Finders Keepers* by Stephen King. The crime novel is a calculated move on my part. Anything else, and Gigi would start reading it. I probably could be more discreet, but I need this like I need air. Flipping the pages, I stop at the familiar page seventy-three—bookmarked by my trusty razor blade and flecked with a bloodied thumbprint.

I lie in bed and slide down my basketball shorts. The lines have somewhat faded now. They used to be red and angry, now some are brown, some are raised, but most are only two shades darker than my skin color. Time did them good. Not adding new ones did them well. I was starting to be happy a few months ago, right around the time graduation rolled around and I thought I'd be leaving Marble Crest and all that garbage behind me. I thought I didn't need to do this anymore.

I scoff at myself remembering how stupid I was. Thinking that I get to start fresh in college. That I get to fix my relationship with Gigi and Luke, the two most important people to me that I've pushed away.

The blade slices my skin open, making way for blood to drip on the new sheets that Mom picked out for me. Laying my head on the pillow, I hiss in both pain and relief once I feel the burning sting. As I close my eyes, my mind replays the memory of today's events—when I met him.

"Fancy seeing you here, Palmer." The familiar voice that's taunting me freezes me in place. Turning off the faucet, I lift my head up to face the mirror. I don't need to see his reflection to know who it is. Zachary Landon.

"What the fuck are you doing here?"

"I go here," he sneers. His eyes are dark with rage that's all directed toward me, Zach pushes himself off one of the bathroom stall doors and makes his way to me. "You see, when your son of a bitch daddy ruined my family, he destroyed my dad. Now thanks to you, I can't afford the tuition to go to any other school. This shithole was the only place offering me a football scholarship."

"For the last fucking time, Zach. I didn't fucking do anything. And it's not my fault that your mom couldn't keep her legs shut." Regret instantly washes over me once I realize what I've said, but after a whole year of this crap, my sympathy for Zach has diminished to zero.

He puffs his chest, and I cackle. It's funny that he thinks I'd be intimidated by him. We're practically the same height and equally wide.

"I'm going to continue to make your life a living hell, Andrew. Your dad might be untouchable, but you're not."

"Do your worst," I say as I bump his shoulder and walk to the door. Not like he hasn't done it, anyway.

"Saw your girlfriend yesterday." My hand stays glued to the knob. "Such a shame that the basketball team and football team at Marble Crest never hung out together, otherwise I'd have spent lots of time with her."

My body starts trembling with anger, remembering the things he said he'd do to Gigi. Zach tried a lot of shit in high school to break me. At some point he figured out that my weak spot was Gigi. And then he pushed, and pushed, and pushed, causing me to reach a tipping point. I broke. I'll never forget the smug winning look on his face when I fell for his trick.

"Stay the fuck away from Gigi!" I bellow, turning around. "She has nothing to do with this."

The fucking tool shakes his head and smirks at me. He finally got his wish. I took the bait. "Oh, but she does. You know that as well as I do." He closes the gap between us by pointing his index finger to my chest. "You beat me up after we played against Kinsdale Springs. Coach benched me for the next game when he saw me. Scouts came to the game after that, you know. Me being here?" Zach pauses to let out a maniacal laugh, and I wonder who he's hurting more with this conversation, me or him. "It's all your doing, Palmer. Had you not done that, maybe I would've gotten better offers."

"You told me you were going to fucking steal her from me and tell her lies about me, you asshole."

"And maybe I still will," he says, smirking. "We share the same hallways now. Maybe I'll sneak into her dorm. Or maybe, maybe I'll just take her from you fair and square. Why would she want to be with a worthless piece of scum like you anyway?"

He's not going to do shit. He's all bark and no bite. But that's the thing with him. He says the same thing so often, at some point you start believing what he says. I know I do.

It's hard not to after being told for a whole year that I'm a worthless piece of scum.

I'm just like my dad.

The world would be better off with one less Palmer.

I'm nothing.

I will pay for everything.

I'm not important.

I open my eyes and come back to reality once the tenth cut is done, turning my inner thighs into how they used to be before summer vacation. I was hoping to finally go all the way with Gigi and worship her next weekend. Apologize profusely, tell her the truth, and make love to her—right my wrongs. I guess I can kiss that goodbye, there's no fucking way I'm going to let her see me like this. Not that it matters, anyway. I don't think about sex anymore. I haven't even had an orgasm since I lost my virginity to Rachel. Jerking off doesn't feel right when you're disgusted with yourself.

As I clean myself, I let my mind wander to a place I haven't let it in a while.

Would Mom be sad if I fell off the face of Earth? Probably, but I read a lot of parents get divorced when they lose a kid. Maybe that'll be the push she needs, because I'm fucking sure my pathetic excuse of a dad will never tell her the truth.

Would Gigi miss me? A part of me wants to say yes, but a part of me knows I've hurt her. So much. I betrayed Gigi in the worst way, and for what? Because I got all drunk and riled up and wanted to prove a point? I don't fucking deserve her.

And Luke? He probably hates me by now. I pushed him away because he's the only person who knows me from the inside out. He's my best friend. I can't have him finding out about Dad. Luke idolizes Michael Palmer as if he was Jesus himself. I don't want him to know about Zach giving me a hard time, as well. He'd think I was a pussy. Struggling over one guy who can't handle the fact his mom cheated on his dad. Luke had it worse than me, way worse. That dude is tough as nails. I never understood why people always think I'm better than Luke. I'm the wrong Palmer boy to be put on a pedestal. He's the one who's going to bring pride to the family name; he's the only one who can at this point. I hope he does.

I smile when I remember the first time I met Gigi. Luke had it out for her. He hated her guts. He probably still does. I wonder what would happen to them if I wasn't here anymore. With Gigi always spending most of her holidays in New York, their strongest link is not their parents—it's me. Would they finally be friends? Would they lose contact completely? Would they miss me? Would they bond over me being gone?

A chuckle comes out of me when I grab my phone to see both Luke and Gigi texting me, asking me where I'm at. *Wouldn't it be hilarious if they started dating?*

Lying back on the bed, I close my eyes and rub my temples.

Hang on a little longer, Andrew. For Mom. For Luke. For Gigi. Not until you tell Mom you love her. Not until you tell Gigi you're sorry for wasting her time. Not until you tell Luke to keep pushing through life.

The end, for now.

If you enjoyed the story and would like to support me, please consider leaving a review on Goodreads and Amazon. As a new indie author, I need all the social proof that I can get to show that my books resonate with readers. Thank you so much!

While you are waiting for the second book in the installment, check out the blurb for Always You, Again and Again—an angsty, second chance romance that I wrote (available on KU).

Always You, Again and Again

Broken once, broken twice - maybe the third time's the charm?

Nick has been a part of my life for as long as I can remember.

Riding our bikes together, misspelled birthday cards, innocent declarations of love... we lived in a fairy tale, our own little bubble. So when he moved continents away, it felt like he took a piece of me with him.

Then he came back in senior year, and we continued where we had left off, promising each other forever this time. But nothing ever goes as planned, and we quickly realized that we weren't the cheerful, carefree kids we used to be.

When life broke us in ways we thought weren't possible, I had to leave Nick behind.

Nick was my first love, but will he be my last?

Always You, Again and Again is a second-chance romance book that is filled with angst. This love story features two star-crossed childhood sweethearts and their search for a seemingly impossible happy ending.

Acknowledgments

I can never thank my sister-in-law, Adrienne, enough for supporting me. You are truly the best.

Hannah, my lovely alpha reader, editor, hype girl, part-time therapist, and full-time recipient of my incoherent midnight voice note rants... Thank you so much for existing. I really lucked out when I met you.

To Katie, my proofreader, thank you so much for polishing my book (and for your patience).

To Nikki, thank you for designing my book covers. You bring my stories to life.

To my street team, why you even agreed to support me is still beyond me. I met all of you when I had almost zero followers and no book to my name. Thank you so much for taking a chance on me. I owe every single sale and KENP page read to you girls.

To my beta readers—Mackenzie, Kelsey, Sophia, and Kaitlin— I cherish every single comment and feedback that you have given me. Thank you so much for highlighting potential quotes. They have helped me so much with my marketing.

To Ellie from Love Notes PR, thank you so much for helping me with the ARC sign-ups. Sorry for all my dumb questions.

To my ARC readers, thank you, thank you, and another round of thank you for taking a chance on my book.

To my little Ines, thank you so much for letting Mommy skip bedtime and work at night.

About the Author

Hi! I'm the author that goes by the pen name Sara Amanda. If you have made it this far, that means you read my book until the end. Thank you very much for finishing the story :)

Now, a little bit about me: Although I have Asian roots, I have been living in Germany for more than a decade now. I have moved around a lot in my short life, and at some point, decided to settle down here with my husband, child, and our greyhound. When I'm not creating the next book boyfriend, I like to spend my time eating, cooking, and baking. I love food!

I mentioned above that I have lived in different places. This is why when you read my book, you might realize that the characters don't always stay in one city. I love writing stories where the characters feel lost, only to find themselves again in the people they love and the memories they have. Home is where the heart is.

Imprint

According to Section 5 of the German Telemedia Act (TMG)

Author Sara Amanda
c/o IP-Management #34137
Ludwig-Erhard-Straße 18
20459 Hamburg

Printed in Great Britain
by Amazon

58471807R00136